THE NEW GULLIVER AND OTHER STORIES

By

BARRY PAIN

THE NEW GULLIVER

CHAPTER I

(The first few pages of the account of his travels by Mr Lemuel Gulliver, junior, have unfortunately been damaged by fire and are for the most part illegible. They contain reference to a sea-fog and to a shipwreck. He appears to have escaped by swimming, and his record of the number of days he spent in the water and the distance covered verges upon the incredible. His statement that he lived principally upon the raw flesh of those sharks which made the mistake of attacking him will also be accepted with reserve by those who remember the latitude in which the Island of Thule is traditionally placed. The legible and consecutive manuscript begins with his arrival at the island.)

I now wrung the water from my clothes as well as I might, and spread them on the rocks in the sun. After an hour, perhaps, I was so far recovered from my exertions that I thought I might now see what manner of island this was to which my ill-chance had brought me. Donning my clothes again I climbed up the low cliff.

The land that now lay before me appeared to be for the most part flat and bleak in character. There were long stretches of sand and coarse grass, and here and there a group of stunted shrubs. Presently, in the far distance, by the aid of my perspective-glass, I made out several cultivated plots, but nowhere could I detect any building which might serve as a human habitation. At one point, which I guessed to be about two miles away, a column of smoke arose, as if from the interior of the earth. This I imagined to be of volcanic origin, but it puzzled me not a little that the land should be under cultivation and that yet I could find not so much as a single house or cottage.

So intent was I upon my survey of the distance that I did not note the approach of a human being until I heard the footsteps close beside me. I speak of it as a human being, but in many respects the creature differed from humanity as previously known to me. Particularly noticeable was its manner of progression. It walked very slowly and laboriously on all fours, the arms being longer and the legs shorter than in the normal man. Its body was clothed in two garments of a thick grey woollen material, and loose boots with tops of a similar material, but with leather soles, were worn both on the hands and feet. The size of the head was disproportionately large and seemed too heavy for the slender neck. It was bald save for a fringe of scanty grey hair. Large spectacles of high magnifying power distorted the eyes, and the toothless mouth was absurdly small. The grotesque object was more likely to inspire laughter than fear, for the body was small and its movements slow and feeble, but indeed it showed not the slightest sign of hostility.

"I see," said the creature, "that you are from the old world. Who are you?" He spoke in a gentle voice and with an accent not unlike that which we call American.

"My name is Lemuel Gulliver, a shipwrecked mariner, at your service. Will you tell me what island this is on which I find myself, and to whom I am speaking."

"The island is Thule—Ultima Thule—the one spot of earth that has emerged from barbarism. Chance has done great things for you in bringing you here."

He slipped one hand out of its boot, removed his big spectacles, and blinked his weak eyes. I watched him narrowly. His face was hairless. It might have been the face of an old woman or of an old man. A look of cunning now crept over it.

"I think," he said, "that I grasp your difficulty. You may speak of me as a man; but for beings of the first class, to which I belong, sex is abolished. It was perhaps the worst of nature's evils that our triumphant civilisation in the process of centuries overcame."

"But in that case," I said, "your race, or that class of it to which you belong, must be rapidly dying out."

"It is undoubtedly dying out," said the strange creature with a complacent smile, "but less rapidly than a barbarian would suppose. Increased knowledge has brought with it increased longevity. I am myself one hundred and ninety-two years of age. The end must come, of course, but after all, why not?"

As I looked at him I did not from the æsthetic point of view see why not. The creature had replaced the spectacles now, and lay at full length on the sand, as if wearied by the standing position. He went on speaking:

"Death in the individual is, of course, to some extent a confession of failure. It means inability, mostly due to ignorance, to adapt oneself to one's environment. Death of a race may be quite a different matter—an exhaustion of utility. However that may be, it is clear that the last of us to survive will represent the highest possible development of human potentiality. I speculate sometimes on the question of who the ultimate survivor will be. It may possibly be Professor YM6403 of the Outer Office. Some think so. I believe he thinks so himself. On the other hand, I may be the last survivor. However, there are still some thousands of us in existence, and for the present these disquisitions may appear to you idle."

My clothes were damp and I was chilly, hungry, and tired. His jabber about professors and survivors had no interest for me. I ventured to point out to him that I was at present in urgent need of rest and refreshment.

He rose on all fours again, and did so with extreme awkwardness. "True," he said. "I will attend to it. We are hospitable people, though it is seldom that a stranger visits us. I will proceed at once to conduct you to my house."

"Your house? I fear that must be at some great distance, for there is no house in sight."

For a moment he looked puzzled, and then light dawned again in his short-sighted eyes.

"I see your mistake," he said. "You come from the old world, where the old type of house is still in existence. The history of the old world is the special study of my friend, the Professor. But of course there is general knowledge that every educated being may be supposed to possess, and I know the type of house you mean. I have seen pictures of it in the museum. Now in Thule, when many centuries ago aviation became the cheapest and most popular form of transit, it also became obviously impossible that we should have houses above ground. Aviation is a source of danger to such houses, and the houses themselves were dangerous to the aviator. Our buildings are all subterranean. We avoid danger of every kind. We dislike risk. You cannot see my house to which I am taking you, but as a matter of fact it is less than a quarter of a mile away."

He went so slowly that I had to abate my usual pace, lest I should outstrip my guide. As he moved, he looked a little like a very small tired elephant.

"Aviation," I said. "I suppose that with you that has been carried to a great point of perfection."

"On the contrary," he said, "it is superseded. It is a back number. We no longer use it. But we have seen no reason to change our style of domicile, which possesses many advantages."

"And what is it?" I asked, "that has superseded aviation?"

"It is the power to dissipate and subsequently reconstruct identically at some different point the atoms of any organism or group of organisms."

"I don't think I understand," I said.

"It is natural that you should not. However, here we are at my house."

It looked to me rather as if we had come to an ordinary well, the interior of which was occupied by a spiral descending incline.

"You will observe," he said, "that when I am weary of exertion and return to my house, I descend. In the old type of house it was customary to ascend."

I should calculate that we descended some thirty-five or forty feet below the surface. At this point we were confronted by a perfectly ordinary door with a brass knocker on it and an electric light above it. On the door were painted the letters and figures MZ04. He opened the door with a small latchkey, which he produced from one of his boots. The keyhole and the handle were placed at such a height that it was easy for him to reach them without assuming the erect position. We went through into a small hall, brightly lit and containing no furniture but a door-mat, on which my guide wiped his four boots carefully. He then requested me to come with him into the dining-room, as indeed I was by no means reluctant to do.

On entering this room, however, I was disappointed, for it bore no resemblance whatever to a dining-room, and there was no look of good cheer about it. Its walls were lined with shelves, and the shelves were filled with numbered bottles containing what looked like small pills. In the middle of the room, immediately under the light, was a low table, on which were a row of small aluminium cups and a leather-bound book. There was no other furniture of any description.

"You are looking for a chair perhaps," said my host presently. "We have none. To stand erect on the feet is a precarious position, and to sit is hardly less precarious. We avoid all risk. On all fours or in a recumbent position one is safe. However, if you would like to sit on the floor, pray do so, while I make up the prescription which you require."

I sat down on the floor, which was very hard and discouraging. I did not greatly like that use of the word "prescription," and my inner man cried rather for butcher's meat than for chemist's stuff. However, a man must take his adventures as he finds them.

My guide slipped his hands out of his boots and consulted the volume on the table. "From long use," he said meditatively, "I know most of the numbers by heart; but I cannot recall what is taken for a chill caused by prolonged submersion in sea-water. I have never had occasion to use it. Ah, here we are! Number one hundred and one."

He took down the bottle which bore that number, and dropped one pill from it into an aluminium cup. I noticed that the shelves were all placed low on the wall. But indeed the whole of the appointments and furniture of the house was adapted for beings who used the quadrupedal position. I noticed, moreover, both now and afterwards, what very little furniture there was in these houses. The hatred of superfluity was a marked characteristic of the people of Thule.

My host took down one bottle after another from the shelves, talking as he did so. Each bottle had an ingenious stopper, which allowed one pill, and only one, to fall out each time that the bottle was reversed.

"I have never eaten shark, cooked or uncooked," said my host, "but I should imagine that a diet confined to this meat would give an excess of nitrogen. We correct that with one of number eighteen. To this I add our ordinary repast—numbers one, two, and three—a corrective for exhaustion from number sixty-four, and a pill of a narcotic character from sixty-eight."

He handed me the little aluminium cup with the pills in it. "I think," he said, "that is all you require."

"I am extremely thirsty," I said.

"No civilised man eats and drinks at the same time." He whisked down another bottle and dropped one more pill into my cup. "You will find," he said, "that little addition will remove all sensation of thirst. You shall drink when the right time comes."

I took my pills obediently and was now conducted by him into a much smaller room on the same level. I afterwards saw other subterranean houses in the island. They were all alike in plan, and the rooms were all small and so low that when I stood erect I could easily touch the ceiling with my hand. The total absence of decoration, and the simplicity and scarcity of the furniture, were not specially characteristic of my host. Æsthetic pleasure was very slightly appreciated by any of the first-class beings in Thule.

A pneumatic mattress lay at one end of the room which we had now entered, and there were two dials on the wall, each provided with a moving hand. There was no other furniture of any kind.

"There is your bed," said my host. "Now sleep."

"I should hardly have called it a bed," I said dubiously.

"It is not the barbarian idea of a bed. We abandoned bed-clothes of every description long ago. They are not hygienic. All that is necessary is to raise the temperature of the room in which the sleeper lies. This you can easily do by altering the hand on the first of these dials, which controls the heat. It stands at present at fifteen. When I sleep I generally put it up to twenty. We will try it at twenty, and you can advance it farther if you find yourself chilly. The other dial controls the lighting and gives you five degrees of light down to absolute darkness."

"I wonder," I said, "if I might have my clothes dried. They are still damp, I fear."

He looked at my garments with marked distaste.

"If you will put them outside the door," he said, "I will see that they are thrown into the refuse-destructor, and will order proper clothes to be provided for you in their place. You will sleep for one hour, and shortly after that I shall return. By the way, how comes it that you speak our language?"

"I speak English," I said.

"English," he said meditatively. "English. I have heard that word somewhere. No, don't explain. I can easily obtain the information."

He now left me. I put the hand on the heat dial at twenty-five. Although I had no clothes of any description, I felt pleasantly warm, and in spite of the excitement caused by the novelty of my experience, I soon fell asleep. This may be ascribed either to the fatigues I had undergone or to the potency of the drugs administered to me.

CHAPTER II

When I awoke, it seemed to me that I must have slept for some six or eight hours, yet it had been but one hour only. I felt perfectly refreshed and well. I had shut off nearly all the light before falling asleep, and I now groped my way to the light dial and moved the hand round until the room was brightly illuminated. The silence of the place was remarkable; it was almost as if I had been in an uninhabited house. I opened the door of my room a little way, and was pleased to find a bundle of clothes awaiting me outside. I brought the bundle in and investigated it. At first sight it looked as if some mad and malicious tailor had made two pairs of trousers out of a material suitable for an overcoat. The reason of course was that the suit had been made with a view to the conformation and habits of the natives of this curious island. They wear two garments only, and therefore require them to be of considerable thickness, and their arms are of about the same length as their legs. (The difference in our own case is much less than most people imagine.) I soon put the two garments on, and found that they fitted me well enough if I rolled back the sleeves to leave my hands free. I was also provided with a pair of boots similar to those my host wore. They were too large for me, but could be kept on by a buckle and strap fastening at the ankle.

I now made some examination of the room itself. The walls and ceiling were covered with a hard shiny substance, which I at first thought to be paint, but afterwards decided to be of the nature of our water-glass. The usual right-angles between floor and walls and ceiling were in every case softened into a curve, which I recognised to be an advantage from the point of view of cleanliness. The floor itself was covered with the same material as the walls and ceiling, but in this case had a minute corrugation all over it, to prevent slipping. In the middle of the floor was a small grating, about one foot square. As I inspected this, a fan below it began to whirl rapidly, but without the slightest sound. As I was looking at it my host knocked and entered. I was pleased to see that he brought with him a sealed bottle and two aluminium cups that would have held about half a pint apiece.

"We now drink," he said briefly.

"An excellent idea," I began, but he immediately bade me to be quiet, saying that it was not customary to talk while drinking was in progress.

He divided the contents of the bottle (not quite fairly) between the two cups. He gave himself the advantage of the choice and finished his drink at a draught. I followed his example and found that I was drinking distilled water. At this I was somewhat disappointed, but the more disposed to forgive him for the injustice of the division.

"And now, my friend," he said, "we can talk."

"Then," I replied, "you will perhaps tell me what is the reason for the custom which prevents you from taking your drink in a sociable manner. In the country from which I come we like to sit and chat over our glass."

"So it was here also in the dark ages," said my host. "At that time our drink was for the most part of an alcoholic character, and it was found that the more one talked, the more one drank; and the more one drank, the more one talked. It was a vicious circle of foolishness and ill-health, and the practice was made illegal. Alcoholic drink is quite unknown now among the first-class beings of Thule. But the custom of not speaking when one drinks, although we now only drink water, still remains. It is one of the many instances in which the ritual has survived the religion."

I pointed now to the grating in the floor. "A ventilator, I suppose."

"Exactly. It is actuated once every hour for two minutes. It draws out carbon dioxide, which being heavier than air is in the lower part of the room, and at the same time draws in fresh air through the corresponding grating in the ceiling, which communicates with a shaft to the open. The great point about it is that it is absolutely noiseless. Our study of longevity has shown us that irritation is one of its deadliest enemies. The noise of an electric fan is irritating, especially in a bedroom. I dare say the crude appliances you have in the old world still whir or clatter."

"I notice that all your electric lights are fixed in the ceiling itself. Is there any reason for this?"

"Naturally. Anything which hangs may subsequently fall. We do not court dangers. It is curious that you should mention it, because I was speaking of this point only last week to my friend, the Professor. He showed me a picture of an old-world chandelier. He also told me it was the custom in England and other uncivilised parts of the world to daub oil-paints on a piece of canvas. This was surrounded by a heavy frame and was suspended on walls. It was called a framed picture. You will find nothing so reckless here. By the way, I have found out about England. I cross-spoke to the Outer Office, and they told me it was a piece of land at the back of Scotland."

I found later that "to cross-speak" meant in Thule to send a wireless message.

"The mention of the Professor," my host continued, "reminds me that to-day is his birthday and mine. On this day I generally make him a ceremonial visit, and I shall be pleased to take you with me. As a specimen you will interest him."

"Might I ask what you mean by the Outer Office?"

"The Central Office deals with utilitarian knowledge and is separated into Controls. I, for instance, am at the head of the Heat and Light Control. The Outer Office deals with academical knowledge, and our friend is the Professor of Old-World History. The Inner Office decides questions of justice. But there is no time just now to explain our simple constitution to you. We should be starting for the Professor's house."

"One more point," I said. "May I ask your name? I should have done so before."

"We do not have names. Beings of the first class have a distinguishing formula, and only use names for plants and the lower animals. The second-class beings, the workers, may possibly use names among themselves, but of that I have no knowledge. My own distinguishing formula is MZ04, and as no two people have the same formula, much confusion is prevented. By the way, your hair is untidy."

"Naturally," I said. "I was going to speak of it."

"And your hands are not clean. That is as it should be. You are now ready to pay a ceremonial call. You perhaps don't understand. All our houses are on the same pattern, and each is provided with a fitted room for the purposes of the bath and the toilet. But when we pay a ceremonial call, it is our invariable custom to do so in a soiled and dishevelled condition. On arriving we make ourselves clean and tidy in our host's toilet-room. This is done by way of compliment. It implies that he possesses conveniences which we do not."

"It seems to me singularly foolish, if I may say so."

"From one point of view all compliments are foolish, but from the point of view of longevity all compliments are wise. They have a slightly emollient effect. We recognise this so much that we even employ at times professional optimists."

"Won't you tell me about them?"

"It is a very simple matter. If a being of the first class gets worried and depressed, he knows that this is lowering his vitality and lessening the period of his life. This knowledge only tends to increase the worry. He therefore sends at once to the Central Office for a professional optimist. The optimist comes and talks. He slightly emphasises all that is most favourable in the being's circumstances. He dwells on the strong points in his character. He listens to his stories. He shows himself impressed by his abilities. We have but a few of these professional optimists, and they are extremely well paid—that is to say, their power of ordering from the Central Office is very considerable."

"Some of this seems to me rather childish," I said. "And some of it I do not understand."

"You, a barbarian, can hardly be expected to grasp at once the refinements of a higher civilisation. You will do so gradually. Now, please, I have only just time to see the Professor before I keep my appointment at the Heat and Light Control. Come along, please."

We passed up the spiral slope, my host going very slowly and breathing heavily. The Professor's house was scarcely a hundred yards away, and I think we took nearly five minutes to get to it. The outward appearance was precisely similar to that of the house we had just quitted. When we reached the outer door my guide knocked once. The door immediately opened, as if of itself, and we passed into an empty hall. From this a door led us into a large room devoted to the purposes of the bath and the toilet. I subsequently found that in all these subterranean houses this room was the largest. I remarked to my guide that no servant had admitted us, and there seemed to be no one to introduce us into the presence of the Professor.

"There are no servants," said my companion. "We have the second class, the workers, but we should not admit them to live in our houses. We have so far simplified life that one being can very well look after one house, his own. As a matter of fact two second-class beings are sent from the Hygienic Control of the Central Office every morning to clean each house, but it is a question whether this should continue. We are discussing it. It looks just a little like luxury, and luxury is dangerous to longevity. Why should we have a servant to announce us? If the Professor knows the visitor, it is not necessary. If he does not know him, the visitor can supply the information just as well as the servant. If the Professor had not wished to receive, the outer door would not have opened."

We did not find the Professor in the first room we entered, but in the dining-room, where he was taking pills out of one of those small aluminium cups. He went on taking his pills and we watched in solemn silence until he had finished. In appearance the Professor closely resembled my guide, but his fringe of hair was darker and more abundant, and something in his face seemed to betoken a love of study rather than high practical ability. I now witnessed another curious piece of etiquette.

"I hope you are ill," said my guide genially.

"Wrong absolutely," said the Professor, "but I trust that you yourself are suffering from some malignant disease."

"Nothing of the kind," said MZ04.

Subsequent inquiries showed me the reason for this. The principle was that the guest should take the earliest opportunity to make his host feel in a superior position. Therefore etiquette required the guest to arrive unkempt, as if he did not possess the conveniences which his host had at his disposal. It also required him to make an obviously false statement as to his host's health, in order that his host might have the power of correcting him. A well-bred host, such as the Professor, immediately replied by giving his guest a similar opportunity to correct and in consequence to feel in the superior position.

They now exchanged rather ponderous compliments on their respective birthdays. But in spite of their politeness I somehow got the impression that these two beings were in strong antagonism to one another, and that however much the emotions might be discouraged in Thule, feelings of jealously still existed.

"On this auspicious occasion," said the Professor, "it is generally my custom to make you some slight offering. I have placed a power to read a manuscript to your order at the Central Office."

"I thank you sincerely," said MZ04. "I had intended to do the same thing, but I think I have found something even more to your taste." He pointed at me with his booted hand. "Here," he said, "is rather a curious thing that I have found. You make a study of the old world and might be interested in it. I have no use for such curios myself and am happy to present it to you. In many respects—notably in its foolish use of the erect position—it resembles our second-class beings, but I believe it to be a genuine old-world relic."

"I am of the same opinion," said the Professor, "and I am obliged to you for your generosity. Can it talk?"

"Fluently," said MZ04, "but with a bad accent."

I now said very decisively that I was a free man, that I did not belong to either of them, and that I absolutely declined to be handed as a slave or a chattel from one to the other. I repeated this in varying terms more than once. They took not the slightest notice of it, but waited patiently till I had finished.

"I am busy to-day at the Heat and Light Control," said MZ04. "I fear that I must now leave you."

"Going to walk?" asked the Professor.

"No. I have taken my exercise for to-day. I shall disintegrate."

Even as I looked at him, his substance became a smoky shadow, shimmering and vibrating. It grew rapidly fainter and fainter until it had vanished altogether.

CHAPTER III

"And now," said the Professor, "before we go any further there is one point on which I wish to be assured. You came from the house of MZ04 just now?"

"I did."

"Did you observe in him as he came up to slope from his front-door any tendency to puff and blow?"

"He certainly did seem slightly short of breath."

"Poor fellow! Poor fellow! It breaks my heart to hear it. I don't give him another hundred years to live. Sad that so intelligent a being should be snuffed out like a candle."

The Professor did not look in the least as if it had broken his heart. So far as I was able to judge he seemed rather pleased than not.

"That being settled," he continued, "I may now devote myself to you. You made some protests just now, based, as most protests are, on ignorance. You are not going to be a slave. You may regard me as your host. I shall treat you as a guest and I shall look upon you as a curiosity. Tell me at once what I can do for you."

"I want to know where I am. I want to know the history of this place—the meaning of first-class and second-class beings—how sex came to be abolished —what is implied by a power of order from the Central Office. I have been here but a few hours and I find everything puzzling and incomprehensible."

"This," said the Professor, "is Thule. I cannot give you its exact geographical relation to the world, for it has no geographical relation. How do you imagine that you came here?"

I gave him some account of the shipwreck and of my fight with the sharks, showing him in proof my large clasp-knife, which, together with my perspective-glass and some other trifles, I had found means to secrete in the clothing provided for me by my former host.

"I have no doubt," said the Professor, "that you speak with sincerity. But you are wrong. That is not how you came here. Nor shall I put you in possession of the actual facts, or you would be able to use them to ensure your return. You are not a prisoner, but at present I wish to detain you. And now, if you will, I will give you roughly and in as few words as possible a sketch of our history and constitution. This being in the nature of a lecture, I shall lie down. It is the custom in this country for every lecture or public speech to be delivered in a recumbent position, the greatest physical ease being consistent with the greatest mental concentration. Come to the sleeping-room."

He led the way to a room provided with a pneumatic mattress. It was in all respects the counterpart of the room I had seen at my former host's house. He stretched himself on this mattress, and as there was plenty of room I saw no reason why I should not do the same. He noticed it and approved.

"You are wise," he said. "Your carcass will now cease to attract your attention and you will be able to attend to me."

He lay on his back with his eyes fixed on the ceiling, and his two long arms crossed over his protuberant stomach. Presently he began to speak in a solemn and magisterial voice, as if he were addressing a large class. I did from time to time interrupt him with question or remark, but have not thought it worth while to place such interruptions on record.

"To understand the conditions of Thule at the present day we must go back to the great social upheaval of centuries ago. At that time the equality of all men was claimed and the community of property. Successful agitation backed by armed force carried the matter. Community of property does to some extent remain to this day, although a more civilised view of the value of property is now held by us. But within a very few years of the social upheaval the fallacy of universal equality declared itself. It is a rare thing for two men to be facially alike, and no two men are ever equal in all respects. Such inequalities soon declared themselves. We had on the one side a minority who contributed more to the State in actual benefit than they received from it, and on the other side a majority who received more from the State than they contributed to it. The minority naturally became a discontented class, and healthy discontent produces activity. The majority, getting more than they gave, were quite satisfied with the state of affairs. They babbled of the blessings of an assured democracy. They took no trouble with themselves. They thought they were at the end of the social revolution when they were only at the beginning of it.

"The formation of a secret society, including most of the minority, was the natural result. You must not make the mistake of confusing this minority with the old aristocracy. The old aristocracy was based on lineage and wealth. The minority of which I speak was based on mind. They were the people who could acquire knowledge and could use knowledge. They included in their number some members of the old upper classes, but many also of the old lower classes. The aim of the secret society which they formed was not only the acquisition of knowledge, principally of a practical character, but also the seclusion of it. The members were sworn not to impart the secrets of the society to any of the great but inactive majority. In this secret society we have the origin of what are now called first-class beings. In the glutted and lazy democracy who formed the majority we have the origin of what we call second-class beings—beings who to-day are permitted to acquire no other knowledge whatever than that which is necessary for the work which they do under compulsion from us. At this moment by far the greater number of them are unable to read or to write or to perform the simplest operations of arithmetic.

"It is of course a commonplace of the text-books that no social evolution follows exactly on lines laid down and planned. The secret society, which was known as the Crypt, was formed originally for the purposes of self-defence. The only means by which a few superior beings could protect themselves against the aggression of the many inferior was by the possession of secret knowledge. To take a case in point: improvements of the first importance in the accumulation and transmission of electricity were made by a member of the Crypt whose formula was H401. H401 was called upon to specify and to explain what he had done. He produced a written statement which was from the first word to the last abject nonsense veiled in pompous scientific phraseology. It was accepted as perfectly satisfactory and deposited in the archives. Every electrician—every man of sufficient education to detect the fraud—was already a member of the Crypt. With this came the first inkling of the tremendous power which was now in the hands of comparatively few men. By the simplest dislocation of machinery they could deprive the great majority of light and heat, and could, if they would, choose a severe mid-winter for the operation. Many other secrets of knowledge came into the hands of the Crypt. I will not weary you with a catalogue of them, but I will mention one of which our friend MZ04 gave you just now a practical demonstration. I refer to the power to dissipate and subsequently to reconstruct identically at some different point the atoms of any organism or group of organisms. You saw just now how MZ04 dissipated himself as it were into smoke in order to reconstruct himself instantaneously at the Heat and Light Control, over which he presides. It is a secret of this kind which makes one being the master of many armies. This was realised by the Crypt and a course of offensive action was at last decided upon.

"At this juncture the voice of the Crypt was practically the voice of that extraordinary and commanding personality Q666—a formula that will be for ever remembered in our history. He was not a being of high scientific attainments. His life was irregular. He had neither scruples nor mercy; but he saw clearly the thing to be attained and the means towards it. At his instigation the General National Assembly was declared to be dissolved, and the whole of the second-class beings were enjoined under penalty of death to yield the strictest obedience to the orders of the Crypt as issued.

"The proclamation was received with ridicule by the second class. Democracy had always triumphed and would triumph again. It relied much upon the fact that the army was entirely democratic. That is to say, no officer or man was a member of the Crypt. The army was not deficient in courage. Its officers included even some few men who took their profession seriously. It was confidently anticipated that after a few days of civil war the Crypt would be compelled to submit.

"I have said that Q666 was a being without scruple. His declaration was made in mid-winter and the whole land was ice-bound. And on the night that followed the declaration heat and light were cut off from the dwellings and camps of his opponents. Some thousands died that night and many more in the course of the next few days. The water which they drank was mysteriously tainted and produced death. Their army found no objective for attack, so rapidly, by virtue of that power which I have described, did the members of the Crypt come and go. On the day when the democracy submitted and received the new constitution by which they ranked as second-class beings, they had actually become inferior in numbers to the beings of the first class. The rule which Q666 established remains to this day. Sentimentalists had in the old days clamoured for the abolition of capital punishment. Q666 abolished every other kind of punishment except this. The punishment for idleness after three warnings was death. The punishment for any intentional disobedience was death without any warning at all.

"I have given you quite roughly and simply with little or no detail the story of the struggle between the Crypt and the democracy, ending in the establishment of first-class and second-class beings.

"I have shown how from an attempt to establish universal equality and to abolish all class distinction there came into being two classes between which there was a distinct cleavage—a class of masters and a class of servants. The end of the struggle was only what could have been expected. While all the harnessed forces of wind and tide provided radiance and warmth for the members of the Crypt, their opponents froze in the darkness. The same water that poisoned the democracy that drank it refreshed the masters without injuring them. The old-fashioned disciplined stupid army was powerless against opponents whose mobilisation, swift as lightning, rendered them practically invisible. There is still much to relate to you, but I grow weary of talking. I propose to take you to see my plants."

"Got a nice garden?"

"We have no gardens. I keep my plants as pets here in my house. Without awakening any emotion which might be prejudicial to longevity, they provide a mild interest and a salutary change from more serious occupation. Follow me and I will show you them."

He rose from the mattress and I noticed that he did so with more ease and agility than had characterised the movements of my poor friend MZ04. I followed him to a room so small that it might almost have been called a cupboard. It was intensely lit by a tinted electric light. In it were two tall plants in tubs.

The leaves of the plants were large and of a tropical character. Each had a stem about three feet in height, surmounted by a ball which looked as if it were made of fine silk. The colour of the ball or flower in one case was a peacock-blue and in the other dead black. I noticed a slight movement of the leaves as we entered the room and assigned it to the opening of the door.

"The plant with the blue head is Edward," said my host. "He is rather an affectionate little thing. Observe."

He called Edward twice in a caressing voice, and immediately the stem of the plant bent downwards and the silky blue ball rubbed itself caressingly against my host's cheek. Almost immediately the other plant began to agitate its leaves violently and to waggle its black ball backwards and forwards.

"You observe?" said my guide. "Frederick is jealous."

He gave each of them a little water and we then went back to the sleeping-room again.

"I never saw anything like that in my life before," I said. "Plants with us cannot move of their own volition. They——"

"Surely you mistake," said the Professor. "I am no botanist, but I have made a special study of what went on in the old world, and I think I am correct in saying that there were creeping plants there which moved to find their supports, and plants whose leaves shrivelled up at a touch, and others that actually devoured the insects which formed their sustenance. Almost anything can be done with plants and knowledge. The old world produced many new varieties—some of them of real utility, as for instance the thornless cactus. We have merely gone a little further. We live in solitude and a companion of some kind is a necessity. I think you will find that every first-class being here keeps one or two pet plants."

"You don't keep dogs or cats?"

"We keep nothing which can be both offensive and provocative of strong affection. Cats and dogs, common though they were in the old world, stand condemned under both categories."

CHAPTER IV

"This," said the Professor, "is the hour at which on fine and warm days we go out and bask in the sun. Sunlight is the enemy of disease and the friend of longevity. You would perhaps like to come with me. We shall find many more engaged in the same occupation."

We passed out of the house and up the spiral incline. The scene before me reminded me somewhat of certain stretches of grass in our public parks on a hot day. Here and there on the coarse grass or sand were stretched the grey-clad bodies of beings of the first class. I did not see any engaged in conversation or in reading or even in sleep. They simply lay still in the sun. Some of them had brought rugs with them. One who appeared to be very infirm was carried in a kind of litter by four finely built men who walked erect.

"That," said the Professor, "is the grandson of the great Q666."

"And who are the fine-looking men who are carrying him?"

"Merely second-class beings detailed for the work. Take no notice of them. They will not, of course, venture to remain in our presence."

The four men deposited their master gently on a bed of tufted grass and marched away again without a word. So far as I could compute, there were now some two hundred first-class beings stretched out motionless under the pleasant and vivifying warmth of the sun.

"May we not," I asked as we reposed ourselves, "take this opportunity for some continuation of your lecture? There is still much about which I am curious."

"On what point would you wish me to speak first?"

"I am told that among beings of the first class at any rate sex is abolished."

"Can sex be of interest to any thinking being? It is of no interest at all to me."

"It happens," I said boldly, "to be of the very first interest to myself."

"Very well," said the Professor. "We must withdraw to some distance, so that our voices do not disturb the meditations of others."

I followed him to the spot that he selected. We lay on our backs on the sand and he continued his discourse.

"The practical abolition of sex has with us been a very gradual process extending over centuries. It began with that great social upheaval of which I have already told you. To declare the complete equality of men was to declare the complete equality of the sexes. It ended about one hundred and fifty years ago when the words "men" and "women" ceased to be used by first-class beings, and no distinction of sex was admitted. That I think is all you want to know."

"Pardon me," I said. "You give me no explanation whatever."

"The thing explains itself. Take first the case of a male. You will find in him so many factors mental and physical which belong to the race and so many which belong to the individual. In the case of a male the factors which belong to the individual are very much in excess of those which belong to the race. In the female we find the reverse of this. The factors which belong to the race are in her largely in excess of those which belong to the individual. She is the martyr and trustee of humanity. That was the state of affairs before the great social upheaval of which I have spoken. When women began to mix in every business, profession, and sport, a new type of woman very soon declared itself —unusually tall, flat-chested, small in the hips, destitute of femininity. Briefly, the male type and the female type began to assimilate. Now sex assimilation is the death of sex attraction. All that women spent on their individual development they stole from the race. Marriages became rare and where they existed they were frequently sterile. Gradually, all that made man man and all that made woman woman became rudimentary and atrophied until, as I have told you, one hundred and fifty years ago the distinction between man and woman was abolished. Since that time, and indeed for some ten years previous to it, there has been no instance of birth or marriage or love-making among beings of the first class. The last word of civilisation has been reached. It is a splendid consummation."

"Splendid?" I said doubtfully.

"How can you doubt it? Now that the burden of racial responsibility has been cut off from our backs, our longevity is trebled and more than trebled. This may be assigned in part to our increased knowledge and to the fact that we do no laborious or dangerous work. Laborious and dangerous work is confined to the second class. With them, of course, sex still exists. They are a lower order. They breed up children. When the number of workers is deficient we keep those children. When the number tends to be excessive they are destroyed. Have you never thought into what a quandary racial responsibility led men and women in the dark ages? No married man lived as an unmarried man, no married woman as an unmarried woman. Life became a string of compromises and concessions. There were complicated households with nurseries in them. It must be clear to you that the man who works for six people must work just six times as hard as the man who works for himself alone. Work is dangerous. And if work is dangerous, worry is deadly. Worry is enormously increased where there is any emotional attachment. Look how we have simplified things. To one being one house. The emotions never paid for their keep, and it is civilised to get rid of them. Tears are as little known among the first-class beings of Thule as is the gross and unhygienic kiss. The tortures of modesty do not affect us, for where there is no sex distinction there is no modesty. We are emancipated. We are free. Love implies death. The loveless live long. I may tell you that it is whispered already that we are on the edge of discoveries which may make it possible for us to live for ever."

"Well," I said, "I am not constituted as you are. You would hardly expect me to like what you like."

"I do not expect any man from the old world to be civilised. It would not be reasonable. But what objection can you possibly offer to the state of things among the first-class beings here?"

"Well, to take the first point that occurs to me, it seems to me that you must all be most horribly bored."

"Never," said my host emphatically. "Boredom is the result of living too fast. Those who work too hard or those who enjoy too much must in the intervals of their work or enjoyment be bored. Here we have found by experience the exact pace at which one should live. Every one of the first-class beings has an occupation of some kind for which he was originally fitted by training and is now specially fitted by long experience. Take the Central Office alone. It is divided into many Controls and in each Control there are many sections. The being who made me a present of you, our friend MZ04, is at the head of the Heat and Light Control. In that alone there are forty-two sections and each section finds work for two first-class beings. Love never stimulates us to an excess of work. Love never takes our minds from the thing on which we are engaged. We do what we can do well and we do it under the best possible conditions, and we have no entertainments of any kind. How then can we be bored? I have said enough. Let me meditate."

"There is just one thing more I should like to ask."

"What is your name or formula?"

"My name is Lemuel Gulliver."

"Well, Gulliver, we are kindly and hospitable people. For some weeks I shall be keeping you here and obtaining from you first-hand information on various details of life in the old world. You will be catechised for one hour or so a day. You may take your revenge in advance. I will answer one more question."

"You told me that community of property still practically existed among you."

"It does. Money is not used. In proportion to the work he does a first-class being has the power of ordering what he requires from the Central Office. It is an extremely rare thing for any first-class being to order all to which he is entitled. The wisest are those who reduce property to the barest necessities. At a man's death all that he has reverts to the State. Here we have no appalling families. Here no man has to make provision for prodigal sons and worthless daughters. We are free from the insanity of love and we find it more easy to believe in friendship when friendship must always remain unremunerated."

"And still I do not envy you," I said. "You are not free from all emotions yet. I have already found two in existence among you, and they are two which I do not greatly love."

"What are they?" the Professor asked.

"Fear and jealousy."

"Lie still. You disturb my meditations."

For half an hour he remained silent with his eyes closed, but not, I think, asleep. Then rising suddenly on all fours he said that we would return to his dwelling, take our pills and compose ourselves for the night.

"I would make a request to you," I said. "These pills which you take are wonderful and I have already experienced their good effects. But I do not think I could live upon them. Evolution has brought your digestive apparatus to a pitch of perfection that I cannot hope to possess. What can you do for me?"

"Our workers, the beings of the second class, are accustomed to kill an ox, cut off a piece of it, subject it to the action of heat, and then devour it. They make also a drink which has great attractions for them. It has even led them to disobey, and to disobey is of course to die. I am sorry to mention such filthy diet, but I can think of nothing else. After all it might suit an old-world barbarian."

"I think it might suit me admirably."

"Then I will have second-class rations sent you every day from the Central Office. I will cross-speak the Central Office now in order that they may send you a piece of dead animal before you sleep. The one condition I make is that I shall not see you engaged in tearing it to pieces with your teeth. You will take it in your own room."

"And which will that be?"

"Oh," he said carelessly, "I shall keep you in the cupboard with my two other pets, the plants. You shall have a mattress to lie on."

A few minutes later one of the working class brought a covered tray, deposited it just inside the Professor's door, and departed.

"Your food," said the Professor. "Take it to the cupboard."

I did so with pleasure. I found on the tray a plate of excellent cold roast beef and a knife and fork of rough workmanship and some flat hard biscuits. There was also a bottle containing about a quart of strong old ale. With this I was very well satisfied, and stretching myself on my mattress, for which there was barely room in the cupboard, I composed myself to slumber.

CHAPTER V

I passed a wretched night. I cannot assign this to the small size of my sleeping-room, for I was able to stretch myself at full length and the admirable system of ventilation kept the air always fresh. Such sleep as I had was haunted by dreams in which these four-legged human beings figured largely. Early in the morning I rose and switched on the light, hoping that by pacing my cell or the passage without for a few minutes I might again induce sleep. I saw a strange sight. The silky heads of the two plants swayed gently to and fro continuously. Their leaves rose and fell. Somehow they seemed to suggest to me a caged lion.

"You poor devils," I said aloud.

When I had put out the light and stretched myself on the mattress again I felt the silky head of one of these plants rubbing against my cheek. It startled me at first. I touched it with my hand. It was about the size of a man's fist. I felt its thousand fibres vibrating under my touch.

In the morning another covered tray was brought me, precisely the same as on the previous evening. A bad night gives one little appetite for strong ale in the morning and I begged a drink of distilled water from the Professor. I took that opportunity to explain to him the kind of food that I should require in the future, and to beg for some facilities by which I might cook myself a hot dish. This last he refused, but agreed that my evening ration should be brought to me hot in the future.

I remained with the Professor for fifteen days. Every day for about an hour he catechised me closely on the manner of life in my own country—the old world, as he called it. His knowledge and his ignorance alike amused me. For example, he made a drawing of a hansom-cab which was really fairly accurate; but he was under the impression that hansom-cabs were used in Rome at the time of Julius Cæsar. All his ideas about dates were wrong and confused, and perpetually I had to correct him. He made notes of all that I told him with an ink pencil.

"You are writing a book on this subject?" I asked him one day.

"I am. That is my duty."

"And when will it be printed and published?"

"Upon the defeat of the democracy and the establishment of first-class and second-class beings, the extremely wise course was taken of breaking up all printing-machines and destroying all books, except those copies, mostly manuscript, which were especially selected for the library of the Central Office. We neither print nor publish."

"Why do you call this a wise course? It seems to me the wildest folly. It is to cheap printing and cheap books that the spread of education in my own country has been largely due."

"Undoubtedly. The question of course is whether the spread of education—or rather what you mean by education—is in any way desirable. It seemed to us that one might as well admit children and fools under no supervision to a menagerie of wild beasts and provide them with the keys of the cages. We respect letters. We consider it a dishonour to letters that books should be cheap or easily obtainable. Here it costs a first-class being more to read one manuscript from the library of the Central Office than it would cost you in your own country for a year's subscription to King Mudie."

I informed him that Mudie was not a king and that I did not know how he had got the idea. He accepted the correction as he always accepted every correction, with considerable irritation.

"It seems to me," he continued, "that you use the word education in a very narrow sense. I myself should say that the whole of our second-class beings were educated. Each is trained to the work that he has to do. We have for instance a group of them who are familiar with the ordinary process of plant culture. They can dig, they can prune, they can plant. They have the education for which they are fitted. They are not versed in those extraordinary modifications which can be produced in plants by chemical changes caused artificially in the nature of the sap. That branch is naturally reserved for beings of the first class. They are taught how to weave and how to make the garments which we all wear. They are taught how to clean our houses in the quickest, most silent and most effective manner. Briefly, they do any work which their intelligence and judgment entitle them to do. Beyond that we do not go. We do not give them knowledge which would be dangerous to them and to us. When you return home, my friend, if ever you do return home, preach to your poor benighted people the inequality of man and the advisability of restricting all really important knowledge to the higher grade."

One day while we were chatting about indifferent subjects he mentioned quite casually that he had been cross-speaking the Central Office and that he found that MZ04 had died that morning.

"I am sorry to hear it," I said. "For after all he received me kindly—fed me and clothed me. When is the funeral?"

"Funeral?" said the Professor. "We have no funerals. The body of MZ04 went into the refuse-destructor hours ago. Death is a confession of failure, a sure proof of a blunder somewhere, and therefore ordinary politeness tells us that we should take as little notice of it as possible."

"Who will take his place?" I asked.

"That has already been decided by the Inner Office."

"You had no ambitions in that direction?"

"None whatever. There is no reason why in addition to my present appointment I should not now be holding a post—and a highly placed post—in the Inner Office. It is merely a want of appreciation and, I am afraid I must add, a certain meanness in the minds of some first-class beings which keeps me a humble professor. However, merit will tell; I can trust to that."

The boasted civilisation of Thule had at any rate not extirpated human vanity. The vanity of the Professor was colossal. No compliment was too gross for him to accept with avidity. His nature was indeed very curious and difficult for a simple man like myself to comprehend. In spite of the casual way in which he spoke of death, I was convinced that he lived in hourly dread of it. In spite of the fact that he spoke of every known form of religion as an idle superstition, and professed the most absolute materialism, I think he was unable to disbelieve entirely in the future life. His nerves were not good. Sometimes in the middle of the night he would tap at the door of the cupboard where I slept and ask me to come out and speak to him. There was always some excuse, and I think the excuse was never the true one. The fact of the case is that the extreme solitude in which most of these first-class beings lived had its inevitable effect upon them. They had, as the Professor observed, no entertainments. They had really no social gatherings. Occasionally one friend would pay a brief and formal visit to another friend, but there was nothing beyond that, When they went abroad for exercise or to bask in the sun, they as a rule passed one another unnoticed.

I was myself the reason why for a time the number of visitors to the Professor's house increased considerably. People came to see me, and he produced me and lectured upon me in terms which were sufficiently humiliating.

"Observe," he would say, "the ludicrous smallness of the head and the short and attenuated forelegs. In this respect one might almost believe him to be a second-class being. He is probably, however, a still lower type. The skin is whiter from deficient pigmentation, and the size of the body is smaller than in a second-class male. In the land from which he comes I find that they learn nothing by experience. The child born into the world there naturally adopts the safe quadrupedal position and has the use of its toes. The creature that we have here can do absolutely nothing with his toes and is uncomfortable in the quadrupedal position. In fact, the deformity of his body prevents him from adopting it easily."

At this point in his lecture he would change to a different language and continue. This second language was used by first-class beings among themselves when they wished to say anything without being understood by those whom they considered their inferiors. In the presence of a second-class being it was that language which the first class always adopted. Among themselves and in my presence they spoke English, except on the occasions when they did not wish me to understand them.

I began to rebel against the kind of life which I was leading. I disliked to be made a curiosity and a show of. The monotony affected me. The horrible familiarities of those two plants in my sleeping-room got on my nerves. I began to hint to the Professor that I must have change and more freedom or that the source of his information would possibly be dried up.

"If you became useless to me," he said carelessly, "you would be killed, of course. You would have failed and your body would go into the refuse-destructor."

"Very likely," I said. "But you would not get the information which you want. And you do want it, you know."

That was my trump card. He really did want to acquire all possible information about what he called the old world. In return for this I was always able to obtain concessions, and I did not fail in this case. I told him that I wished to explore the island, to go right over to the other side of it and see the places where the second class lived and the work they did. At first he tried to dissuade me. He pointed out that the distance to the other side of the island was not less than eight miles, and refused to believe that this would not be beyond my strength. He painted in lurid colours the dangers of the mountain which I should have to cross and of the forests which I should find on the other side. I, however, remained obstinate in my purposes and at last obtained his permission to go, on condition that I returned in ten days and that I never spoke with any second-class being whom I might encounter, lest I should inadvertently betray important knowledge to them. This promise I gave readily enough, but, I must confess, with no intention of keeping it. He gave me some further instructions and a pass written with the ink pencil, which he said would entitle me to protection and help from any first-class being whom I might encounter.

Thus then on a fine sunny morning I started out with no more equipment than I could easily carry on my back. The prospect of adventure lured me. For the first time for days I felt in good temper and spirits.

CHAPTER VI

The Professor had been well within the mark in stating that the breadth of the island was not less than eight miles. By sundown I must have covered thirty miles at least and encamped for the night by the side of a swift and narrow stream. I had still the low hill to cross which the Professor had spoken of as a mountain. In a flat country such as Thule, all hills are mountains.

The Professor's mistakes in regard to time and distance interested me a good deal. I could understand that they rendered him professionally unsuitable for the practical work of the Central Office and that they probably helped to debar him from the post which he desired in the Inner Office. It may be, perhaps, that one cannot have an over-development in one direction without a compensating defect in another. The Professor showed the same anxiety to conceal his want of time-sense that an engine-driver might show to conceal his colour-blindness. After all, instances of this want of time-appreciation are common enough among my own people in dealing with the past. One knows the vagueness with which the ordinary man assigns a fact to the sixteenth or seventeenth century—a fact which in reality belongs to the eighteenth. The further back we go the more vague we become. It is difficult for us to realise that the difference between the tenth and eleventh centuries is a difference of a hundred of those very years which we are now living. So far as the present was concerned, the Professor's time-appreciation was clear and accurate enough. He never forgot the hour at which he should take his pills or his siesta in the sun. Watches were unknown in Thule, but there was a clock in every room, and all clocks were wound and synchronised electrically from the Central Office.

I had never been able to persuade the Professor to tell me where the Central, Outer, and Inner Offices were domiciled. I guessed at first it would be where I saw that shaft of smoke ascending when I landed at the island, but afterwards I saw several other similar smoke columns and assigned them to subterranean factories of some kind. But in the course of my day's ramble I came upon many other features that interested me. I reached a long stretch of fields in which a veritable army of the second class was at work. Each field was numbered and seemed to have its separate gang. Each gang was in the charge of one first-class being. As a rule he lay in the sun with one hand removed from the boot and covered with a rubber glove. In this hand he held a thick rod some three feet in length which seemed to me to be made of aluminium. His quick and watchful eyes surveyed the whole of the field, and every now and then he called out an order to some individual labourer. The order was in every case instantly obeyed. In every one of these fields I was challenged by the overseer with a loud "Who are you?" I replied as the Professor had directed me and showed my pass. I was then allowed to go on unmolested. I may even say that I was treated with kindness. One of these beings had water fetched for me that I might drink. Another, astounded by the distance which I had covered on foot, offered to provide four labourers with a litter to carry me, and seemed surprised to find that I really preferred walking. In many of these fields there was grain ready for harvest—of the same kinds, I think, as we have in our country, but with the ears much larger and heavier and of a very dwarf-like habit. I found barley and oats full grown standing scarcely six inches above the ground.

Beyond these cultivated fields was a gently undulating plain, not unlike common land I have seen in England. The bracken was near waist-high, and often I had to force my way through a tangle of bramble and gorse. This part of the country seemed to be entirely deserted, and with no one to direct me I steered by the sun. After some miles of this I came upon a small clump of elm trees and stretched myself in the shade for food and rest.

As I lay asleep I felt a gentle touch upon my shoulder, and opening my eyes I saw one of the first-class beings. I judged him to be one of the overseers, for from one of his big loose boots an aluminium rod projected.

"Who are you?" he said.

I showed him my credentials. He seemed satisfied.

"Go on your way at once," he said, "and bear well to the right, for here you are in danger."

I could not tell what the danger might be, but thought it best to take his advice. As he trotted away from me I fastened up my pack again and slung it on my back, and almost instantly I saw what the danger was. Out from a dip of the land which had concealed them came a herd of about twenty wild cattle. Their size was enormous. The leader, a white bull, scented or sighted me and charged at once towards me. There was but one thing to do. I gripped a low bough and easily swung myself up into the tree, even in the moment of my activity speculating how long I should be kept there and what would happen to the overseer who had spoken to me and was now scarcely a hundred yards distant. The bull paced round and round the tree, pawing the earth and striking the trunk with his great horns. From my perch I could see that the overseer now stood still. He had slipped one hand out of the boot and now grasped that aluminium rod. At that moment the bull sighted him and charged him. The rest of the herd waited huddled and motionless.

When the bull was within about twenty yards of him the overseer raised his hand and pointed that rod towards the beast. There was a flash as of lightning, a loud crackling sound, and the bull rolled over stone dead. The rest of the herd turned tail and galloped off in panic. Without a word to me the overseer replaced the rod in his boot and went on his way.

I could understand now how one of these beings could easily control a gang of thirty or more of the second-class labourers, and could ensure punctual and complete obedience. Yet, grateful though I was to this overseer, I regarded the beings of his type more with wonder than with admiration. They were a selfish and sterile race. Their mode of walking suggested to me too vividly things that I had seen in the great ape-house in Regent's Park. Physically they were not, according to our notions, to be compared with the second class whom they controlled. Those that I saw of the second class were all men of fine stature. Their skins were darker than the European and of a reddish brown. Their faces were handsome, gloomy, and sombre. They seemed more akin to me than did this four-legged thing with the monstrous head and the death-dealing rod in his boot. But as yet I had spoken to no being of the second class. As I passed through the cultivated fields I was all the time under the eyes of the overseers, and deemed it inadvisable to break through the Professor's injunctions.

I saw nothing more of the wild cattle nor of any living being until I reached the stream beside which I camped for the night. I had been told that on the farther side of the hill I should find a forest and beyond the forest the dwellings of the second class and the sea.

As I lay stretched on my rug I heard beneath me a curious rumbling sound and guessed correctly what it might be. It was commonplace enough—an underground train taking the workers back to their homes. Commonplace, at least, in London, but strange in the environment in which I found it. I slept well, as I ever do in the open on a warm night, and in the morning after a refreshing swim in the stream set out to climb the hill.

CHAPTER VII

The air was clear and from the crest of the hill I obtained a fine view. Beneath me lay a forest that covered, I should imagine, some four or five miles. Beyond was the blue sea, and close to the shore what looked like a small town or village of much the same character as we are familiar with in England. These were the first buildings above ground that I had seen in Thule, and constituted the dwellings of beings of the second class.

The attitude of the first class towards the second was rather puzzling. The restriction of the numbers of the workers was quite ruthless. Children that were not wanted were destroyed as we destroy superfluous kittens, fewer girls than boys being allowed to live. The punishment of death was given for any act of disobedience, and even, after due warning, for carelessness and incompetence. But the workers whom I had seen so far—all men—were evidently well treated. They showed no signs of over-work, or under-feeding, or disease. They were tall, stout fellows, all of them, and evidently in fine condition. Not one of them adopted or attempted to adopt the quadrupedal position. They walked erect, and were obviously the physical superiors of their masters. Doubtless utilitarian views had prevailed with the first-class beings, and they gave such treatment to the second class as would ensure the maximum of effective work from them.

The clothing of the workers was of the same thick woollen material as that of their masters, but of a different colour—a reddish brown. The men threw off their upper garment when working in the fields. It will be remembered that on my arrival I was provided by the late MZ04 with grey garments similar to those worn by the first class. I was thus in the nature of an anomaly to everyone who met me. I walked erect and therefore did not belong to the first-class beings. I wore the grey garments, the sleeves of which had now been abbreviated to suit me, and therefore did not belong to the second class. To tell the truth my stature was inferior to theirs, and would by itself have distinguished me.

Standing on the crest of the hill I made my plans. It was in my mind to get away from this island as soon as might be. In a forest of that extent I might easily lie hidden for weeks, and I doubted if, with all his knowledge and cunning, the Professor would be able to find me. Meanwhile I would establish friendly relations with some of the second class. Living as they did upon the sea-shore, I expected that they would have contrived boats for their own use, and thus I might make my escape. I had the whole day before me, and began now to explore the forest, intending to go on to the village on the shore when the workers had returned in the evening.

I followed the course of the stream that trickled down the hill-side. There was no wind, and except for the burble of the stream and the call of the birds all was still in the forest. Here and there the stream broadened out into wide shady pools, where it seemed to me there might be the chance of tickling a trout. Presently I heard below me a loud splashing. The trees and undergrowth were so thick that I could see but a very little way before me. I still followed the stream in the direction of the sound, but I went with extreme caution, taking care that my footsteps should not be heard. I did not know what danger might not be awaiting me below.

Presently I reached the pool from which the sound had come. Peering through the bushes I saw, seated in a dejected attitude by the edge of the pool, a very beautiful woman. In spite of the fact that she had been swimming, and her long dark hair hung dankly about her brown shoulders—wet hair is ever unbecoming to a woman—her beauty was amazing. The brown shoulders peeped from the heavy folds of the garment which she had thrown round her after her swim. It was of the colour prescribed for beings of the second class. The women of that class wear but one garment—a long piece of stuff like a plaid, that they drape about them. As I came into view she started up and gave a scream of terror.

"Do not be afraid," I called. "I mean you no harm. I will not hurt you."

As she looked at me further she seemed reassured. "I thought," she said, "at first that one of the gods had come to take me."

"What gods?" I asked.

"The gods that walk on four legs and against whom no man can do anything. Your dress is of the same colour that they wear."

"I am no god, but an ordinary man enough—a shipwrecked mariner cast up on this island a few weeks ago, and now planning to escape from it again."

"There is no escape," she said mournfully. "The gods know everything."

"Let me come down and speak with you."

"Come," she said. "I am not afraid any more."

"What do you do here?" I asked, as I sat beside her.

"I have fled from death. It was ordained by the gods that I should die at sundown seven days ago. I escaped and hid myself here. But there is no escape really. Sooner or later they will find me. They never fail. In their coming and going they are unseen. Suddenly before you stands one of the gods, and he points his rod at you and you are dead. It is not possible to hide from those whom one cannot see in their approach."

"Has no one ever escaped?"

"Years ago a girl like myself fled to the forest, and for three months in the summer she lived there. It was I myself who found her lying dead. Her garment over her breast was scorched by the lightning of the gods, and her heart was burned within her. It was all one; for in the winter she would have perished of cold and starvation. I love life. I want every day and hour that I can get. But I have no hopes."

"Tell me, what is your name?"

"To the gods I have no name. When I am at work a number is put upon me; it may be a different number every day. Among my own people I am called Dream."

"And why was it that seven days ago you incurred the anger of your masters and were to die?"

"Seven days ago I had the care of a loom. By sundown so much work was to be finished. It is easy work. Our gods never give the women hard work. All the same, that which is appointed must be done. It was just at the beginning of the first spell of hot weather. The forest called me. It was stronger than I was. When I went to my midday meal I slipped into the forest and swam in the pool, and could not go back to the loom again. After that I dared not go back, for those who have disobeyed die instantly. Such is the will of the gods, and we cannot alter it."

"Listen to me," I said. "Those whom you call gods are not gods. They are descended from those who, many years ago, were men and women just as you are. They are not all-powerful. I myself mean to escape from them. Generations of slavery have crushed your spirit, but in the country from which I come there are no slaves. I shall escape and I shall take you with me."

"You are good. I will do as you say. But how can one escape?"

"In the town on the shore I hope to be able to find a boat."

She looked at me with her dark and lustrous eyes wide open in sheer wonderment.

"What is a boat?" she asked.

Her ignorance I found was not assumed. The making of a boat had been prohibited so long by the beings of the first class that now even the recollection of it had passed from the workers. They regarded the sea with terror. It was the grey liquid wall of their prison-house. To touch it was to die. They bathed in the forest pools, and never in the sea. The fish that they ate were fresh-water fish only. Their masters had told them numberless strange lies about the sea.

"Dream," I said, "there is one thing which I cannot understand. You live in daily terror of these people whom you miscall gods. You are fairly well treated, but you are not free. You live as slaves. Why do you tell me, then, that you want every hour and every minute of life?"

She dipped a bare foot in the water below her, passing it slowly to and fro.

"There is always love," she said pensively.

CHAPTER VIII

"What do you know of love?" I asked.

She shrugged her pretty shoulders. "Almost nothing, except of the lesser loves—the love of children, the squirrels in the forest."

"Of parents," I suggested.

"No," said Dream decisively. "You cannot love those whom you do not know."

"But how does it happen that you do not know your parents?"

"How should I? Sometimes for two years, sometimes for three—as the gods decide—the child remains with its parents. After that it is taken away from its parents and brought up by the gods. That is the law."

"But these women who have their children taken away from them—how do they bear it?"

"Sometimes they are so sad that they go away into the forest and eat the nightshade and die. More often they weep for a long time and then they forget. When a thing is the law and it cannot be altered, there are very few who become angry or grieved about it. What would be the use? The gods are very careful about the children, you know."

"In what way careful?"

"If a child is weak, sickly, or misshapen, it is killed instantly. If it is unable to learn how to do any work it is killed. The strong which remain are well treated. For some years they do little work, they are well fed, they are healthy and happy."

I thought of the gangs of magnificently built men that I had seen at work in the fields. I looked at the strong and beautiful girl beside me. The drastic methods of the lords of Thule had at least brought about one thing—the highest possible physical condition of the race.

"Tell me," I said, "do your gods interfere also in the matter of marriage?"

She gazed at me with her sincere and wondering eyes. "What is marriage?" she said, in much the same tone as she had inquired what a boat was.

I told her something of the marriage ceremonies existing in my own country, and she was very much amused.

"But why?" she asked; "that is a very great to-do about very little. If a man loves a woman and the woman also loves the man, what more is there to say? Why write down things in books and call many people to a feast?"

"Dream," I said, "you are an immoral heathen."

"Those also are words that I do not know. You will tell me about them."

I did not tell her about them. I had already been rather struck by the curious simplicity of her own speech. Her phrases were at times biblical, though she knew nothing of any religion, and could not have read a bible if she had possessed one.

"And when, as you say, a man and woman love one another, is it customary with you for them to live together for the rest of their lives?"

Dream yawned. I was wearying her.

"It is so strange," she said, "to have to tell you the things that everybody knows. Also what you ask is so funny. Of course people who love live together. Is not that right?"

I hardly knew what to tell her. She had the innocence of the first garden. After all it may be that the notions of right and wrong which are very properly accepted in my own country are not to be imposed upon every people in every form of civilisation. I did not wish to judge her. I therefore changed the subject.

"This evening, Dream, I want you to take me to that town where you all live. I am going to save you and take you away from this island. To do that I must make a boat or a great raft. I must have men to help me."

"I will take you there if you wish, but if I do I shall die immediately. Every day and every night the overseeing gods go up and down there. It is well known that I left my work at the loom, and that I am to die. The gods have said I am to die, and what they say always happens. Any one of them who saw me in the town would point at me with his death-rod and I should fall. Still, no one has ever escaped, and as I must die anyhow, I will take you to the town if this gives you pleasure."

I could not of course hear of this. My first step to secure her safety could not reasonably be a step which would ensure her death. I asked her, however, how these overseeing gods—the police of the town, as I figured it—would recognise her.

"By the pictures," she said. "They have pictures of every one of us. My picture is put up throughout the town on the walls of houses."

"I see," I said. "If I go to the town at all I will go alone. Shall I be in any danger from your people?"

"None. You wear the grey garments. True, you do not walk like a god, and you suffer from short arms, as I do. But would you be safe from the gods themselves?"

"Yes," I said. "I have something that was given to me to show them. It is a sign that they are not to injure me."

"Injure?" she echoed. "The gods injure nobody. They kill when it is necessary, but they do not injure. If one has a crooked spine, or if one falls sick, or if one has lived too long, or if one refuses obedience, as I have done, then of course they must die. It is the law. The gods themselves have told us that in the old days our forefathers were beaten or shut up in prisons or their goods were taken away from them. This was called punishment. We are free from all that. We have food and shelter, we have light and warmth, we have times of work and times of play. No one punishes us. That is why it is our duty to love the gods."

"Who taught you to say that?"

"They taught it me themselves. It is one of the first things that a child learns. But I grow weary of sitting here and telling you the things that everybody knows. Will you come with me through the forest and down to the shore where the caves are where I sleep?"

I assented. She rose up and draped her garment anew about her. As we walked side by side I asked her if she was not afraid of sleeping in the caves. Surely there first of all the gods would go to look for her.

"No," she said. "Never. No god has ever been inside those caves since the creature came out of the sea and lived there."

"What creature?"

"How should I know? It was more than fifty years ago, and none of us live for fifty years. But I have heard the story as it is told by my people. The creature that came out of the sea was something like a serpent, but larger than all serpents. Those who looked into its eyes died of horror. Two of the gods died. It went away into the caves, and no one has ever seen it again. I suppose it still lives there waiting for something. But it is far away in the very heart of the caves where I never go. If I heard it moving I should awake at once, for I sleep but lightly, and so I should save myself. If I could remain always in the caves I need have no fear of the gods, but one must have the sun, and water to swim in, and food to eat. Is that not so?"

I agreed with her. "But," I said, "in the forest you are in constant danger."

"Only on calm days. When the wind blows the gods will not go into the forest. That is well known, but I do not know what the reason is."

I knew perfectly well. I had already learned their fear of something falling on them. Over-civilisation had broken up their nerves and rendered them flaccid and spiritless. They had no reason to fear the wild cattle with the death-rod in their hands. They had no reason to fear the docile race that they had tamed in ignorance to serve them. But the limb of a tree might fall, or a cave might be haunted. I grew to hate these first-class beings, as they called themselves.

She began now to ask me questions about the land from which I had come, and all that I told her was subjected to her barbarian criticism. She was perfectly shocked at hearing of hospitals, and regarded the whole of the medical fraternity as impious. "If those who are weak and sickly are patched up and made to live a little longer, is there not a danger that they will have children who will also be weak and sickly, and so much more trouble be made? We see that this is so with the beasts that we rear, and the plants that we cultivate. Is it not so with men also?"

I had to admit that it was. But I pointed out to her that in my country we regarded many other things besides physical perfection.

"So I have already observed," she said, with almost embarrassing frankness. "Are the women of your country beautiful?"

"Some of them are very beautiful. Some, I fear, are not beautiful at all."

"Then why do they live? It must be very unpleasant. Are any of them more beautiful than I am?"

"I have never seen anyone, Dream, as beautiful as you are."

"Say that again," she said, "it makes a pleasing sound."

I did not say it again. I felt my responsibilities towards this beautiful but wholly barbarous creature. It seemed to me my duty at the very first to purge her mind of her superstitions about that deformed, intelligent, and learned section of humanity in whose divine character she had been taught to believe.

"If your masters are indeed gods, as you say, why did they not destroy the creature from the sea?"

"Two of them went out to kill it, but they saw its eyes and horror overcame them so that they died. After that they saw that this was a very evil creature, and in their wisdom they left it alone."

"They must be poor creatures to be so easily frightened to death. In my country we could not believe in gods that ever die. Yet the very first of your masters that I saw when I reached this island has since died and his body has been burned."

"His body—yes. But he himself still lives. I was taught these things by the gods when I was a child, and it is wrong of you to try and make me think otherwise."

I began to realise the tremendous strength of early impression. I could call to mind that I had seen evidence enough of it before ever I came to Thule. It seemed almost impossible for me—one man—to fight against this crafty and complex organisation of tyranny and slavery that was here blindly accepted. I turned to another of her terrors—her terror of the sea.

"Do you swim well?" I asked her.

She laughed. "One swims as one walks or runs. Why not? You ask such strange things."

"Very well then," I said, "you shall swim in the sea."

"No. The sea is the evil water. If one had only that water to drink, one would die. Is that not so?"

"It is, but——"

"Very well then. We are rightly taught not to touch the sea. You speak to me sometimes very much as if you were a god, and you boast of freedom, and you have come all the way from a far-off country; but you yourself would not dare to enter the sea."

It was my turn to laugh. "I am going to swim in it this evening," I said.

"I implore you not to do it," said Dream.

"I shall come to no harm."

"You will most certainly die."

"You will see that I shall not."

"It would be a pity, because I myself perhaps may escape death yet for a few days longer, and I might begin to love you."

We had now reached the entrance to the caves.

CHAPTER IX

The side of the brown sandstone cliff was perforated like a gigantic rabbit warren. I judged the cliffs to be natural in character, but in the labyrinth of passages and rooms upon which one first entered, much artificial work had been done. In places columns of brick upheld the roof, and the walls had been trimmed and levelled by a tool. I guessed—for it was a point upon which Dream could tell me nothing—that the lords of Thule had at one time some intention of making use of these natural excavations, and that they had been frightened from their task by the absurd superstition which Dream had recounted to me. I could not believe in the marvellous amphibious monster that had come out of the sea, and for fifty years or more had lived in the heart of these cliffs.

I told Dream of my doubts, but she was not to be shaken. The track of the animal when it went in had been clearly visible, and no track had been found to show that it had gone out again.

"On what then does it live?" I asked.

"Things that it finds in the water."

"But you tell me that it has never gone back to the sea again."

"Never. But far within the caves—much farther than I have ever gone—there is a great lake. It lives there. I will take you to a place where you can hear the roar of the water falling into the lake. Follow me closely or you may lose yourself."

She took me through many winding passages until she reached a point where she knelt and put her ear to the ground. She made me do the same. I could certainly hear the sound of running water below me, but that did not prove the existence of the lake, much less of the monster that was supposed to inhabit the lake. I told her this, and she did not like it.

"When you found me in the forest," she said, "I was very sad because I had spoken to no one for many days, and I was to die and there was no escape. Then because of your companionship and because you seem to hope and to fear nothing, I became lifted up again. It is necessary for you to think as I think, or I shall grow sad again. Therefore you must believe in the great serpent."

"We will not speak of him. Show me where you sleep."

She took me by a passage that rapidly grew narrower until I could hardly force my way into the chamber beyond. It was a simple sleeping-apartment containing a bed of dried bracken and nothing more.

"Yes," she said, "I chose this place because the passage was so narrow and the great serpent which was in the lake was so big. Here he could not get to me."

"And how do you manage about food?"

"I have plenty—far too much. Every night some one or other of my people brings food and puts it at the entrance of the cave. They do not go near to the cave because they believe in the serpent, not being so wise as you are. I would not go into the cave myself were it not that I have to die anyhow."

"But do your gods permit this?"

"I do not know. They do not care to come very near to the caves. I myself think that they do know that food is brought to me and do not wish to prevent it. They have only one punishment. They would not starve me slowly. They would point the death-rod at me and burn my heart out in an instant. But you remind me that I have become very hungry after my swim. You also must think as I do and be hungry too, and we will eat together."

She showed me another room nearer to the entrance where she kept her supplies. They were simple enough. There was a pile of thin sweet biscuit and another pile of dried fruit. This in colour and flavour was like a raisin, but four times the size.

"That grows in the forest," said Dream. "In the autumn when the fresh fruit is ripe it is very good indeed. I shall not live to pick any more of it, and for that I am very sorry."

She was still, I think, rather offended with me for my disbelief in the creature that came out of the sea, but on the whole we chatted amicably enough. I can see now that I did a clumsy thing in thus suddenly and crudely trying to upset a tradition in which she had grown up. It is not perhaps very desirable to shake the faith of anybody in anything, unless that faith be distinctly and immediately harmful. I am a simple seaman and unused to missionary work, and it is small wonder that I bungled it.

After we had feasted, Dream went off to her bed of bracken and I once more climbed the hill to watch the sea. All that afternoon I watched, using at times my perspective-glass, but never once could I make out a sail.

I may admit that my plans were now changed and that the change was entirely due to the strong fascination which Dream had for me—far stronger than I cared to let her know at present. I no longer cared to explore the town or to find out more of the condition of the workers than Dream herself could tell me. I had decided to throw in my lot with her and, if it were possible, to save her from the cruel death with which she was threatened. How I was to do this I did not know. I could only wait and see what chance might offer itself.

I cut bracken for my bed, and laden with this I made my way back to the cave again. There Dream awaited me and all traces of her ill-humour had vanished. I did not insist on my swim in the sea that night, lest it should pain her further. We sat and talked together until the stars came out. It was the first time since I had been on the island that I had looked up at the stars. I could find nothing that I recognised. I wondered where in the world or out of the world I now found myself. The problem did not disturb me greatly. It was pleasant to sit and hear Dream's recital of her story of the squirrel that she captured and tamed. Her voice was curiously soft and caressing.

Soon she went back to her bed and I spread my bracken in the door of the cave and lay down. It was in the night that her people came to bring her food, and I wished if possible to see them and to speak with them.

But this experiment turned out ill. I had slept but an hour when I was awakened by a footfall, and looking out from the cave I saw striding towards me a man who bore a tray on his head. But when he was within a hundred yards of the cave he set the tray down and turned back again. I called out that I was a friend and would speak with him, but I do not think he understood what I said, and the sound of a strange voice filled him with terror. He ran off at the top of his speed.

Early that morning I had my swim in the sea, but on my return I said nothing to Dream about it. I told her, however, how the man had run away when he heard my voice the night before.

"You did not do this very well," said Dream. "You told me that you did not wish to go to the town any more and that you would remain with me. But it seems that I am not enough and that you do wish to speak with others. Very well then. This night I will watch outside the cave and I will go to the man who brings the food and I will bring him in to you. He is, I think, a man who loves me very much indeed."

I told her that I had changed my mind and did not wish to see the man. A brisk wind was blowing and we spent most of the day in the forest together. Again from time to time I scanned the horizon with my perspective-glass, and again with no result whatever. I wondered in what deserted sea this island might be placed. Throughout the day Dream was silent and thoughtful, but she was in no immediate fear, knowing that on such a day her gods would not enter the forest. Next morning I went for my swim in the sea again, and on my return Dream told me that she knew what I had done. She had seen me swimming far out.

"Why did you not tell me you had done this?"

"I feared to disturb your mind."

"I am not a child and am not to be treated as a child. I can think as you think about the sea if I like. I dare do anything that you dare to do."

I told her that I had no doubt of it. Rain fell for the greater part of that day and we remained in the cave talking. She told me of the life she had led and of the laws by which her people were governed.

I have said that I had begun to hate the lords of Thule—the first-class beings as they designated themselves—the gods, as the poor ignorant workers supposed them to be. I hate them still. I despise their sexless emasculate nervousness. I despise their want of the warmer sins and their subjection to the colder. I despise their selfishness even while I admire their wisdom.

Yet, if I am to speak honestly, their despotism—not benevolent and wholly self-interested—produced a finer race of workers than is to be found in my own country to-day. They were better fed, better clothed, better housed. They were healthier—disease was almost unknown—and they were happier. I use the last word deliberately. The cruelty with which they were treated—and to our modern minds it was abominable cruelty—was after all not capricious cruelty. It proceeded on laws as immutable as the laws of nature. The mother of the weakling who saw her child destroyed at any rate knew why; and when the lightning strikes the best and most promising of us we do not know why. Every man was specially trained for special work, and his own inclination was always taken into account; for the greater the inclination, the greater—as a rule—the aptitude. The view taken of women was definitely animal, and only in exceptional cases were women allowed to live beyond the age of forty-five. On the other hand, no woman was worked hard; women who were about to be mothers or had recently become mothers, were treated with a delicate consideration far beyond anything to be found in our Factory Acts; and no woman was influenced in her choice of a mate by vulgar claims of a financial or social character. The children were free from the thwarting and snubbing and the curse of competitive examination which we are pleased to call education. Each child was taught a few essentials very thoroughly. The training was in each case individual and based on a clever study of the child's nature. If reading or writing or arithmetic was unnecessary for the work which the child would ultimately be called upon to do, then none of these things was taught. It might almost be said that the children were spoiled. But they learned early the immutable and inexorable nature of the laws imposed on their race.

Towards the close of this day Dream became once more sad and depressed. Suddenly she rose and said that she was going back to her own people in the town.

"But," I said, "you know that this means death."

"There is one thing worse than death which may happen to a woman. It is useless for you to try to prevent me. If I cannot go to the town, then to-morrow I shall eat the poison berries in the forest."

I had intended, if ever I could find the way, to take Dream back with me to my own country and there to marry her. It seemed to me now that there was no hope of this. I make no defence of what I said or did. I do not know if under those circumstances any defence is needed. But I told Dream that she need not seek the death-rod of her gods or the poison berries of the forest, because the one thing which is worse than death had not happened to her.

CHAPTER X

There followed sixteen days of such great and idyllic happiness that for that alone it seems worth while to have lived my life. Dream lost her terror of the sea and every morning swam out with me. Sometimes we would catch trout in the forest pools, and these I would clean and cook in the manner I had learned in the South Seas, on hot stones and ashes, getting fire from the sun by means of the lens of my perspective-glass. But this we could only hazard on days when the wind blew strongly, lest the smoke of our fire should signal our whereabouts. I was not able to shake Dream's belief in the creature that came out of the sea, but she seemed no longer to have any fear of that or of anything.

"When death comes," she said, "it will come to both of us. Every day is a gain. Yet, when one cannot possibly be happier, it is not hard to die. One has drunk the wine of life."

I had it in my mind to attempt some further exploration of the caves. In this I had been so far prevented by the fact that we had no means of lighting ourselves. It was on the morning of the sixteenth day that I found in the forest wood of a very resinous character which I guessed would make good torches. I got me a store of this and carried it down to the cave, telling Dream what I meant to do.

"I shall go with you," she said. Nor could I dissuade her from it.

We kept a small fire burning at the entrance to the cave that day, and when the sun had gone down we lit our torches from the fire and started off, taking no other equipment than my clasp-knife and a lump of chalk with which to mark our way in the labyrinth.

We soon reached a point where but two roads were left, each so wide and lofty that a coach and four might easily have been driven along it. One of these roads led upwards, and I made no doubt emerged on the farther side of the hill. The other one struck more abruptly downward, and this was the road which we took. Here, if it existed at all, I should find the subterranean lake. As we went on, the noise of falling water became more and more distinct. I was excited by the adventure and eager to see more.

Presently the road widened into a vast hall, so vast that our torches could not illumine the farthest recesses of it. And here it was as well that I looked carefully to each step, for I found myself suddenly on the edge of a precipice. Lying flat on my stomach and holding out my torch, I could see a vast stretch of black water below, into which at one end a cataract thundered. In the middle of this lake there projected something which looked like a smooth boulder of rock. I wondered what it might be.

"We have plenty of torches?" asked Dream.

"Plenty."

"Then we will see what it is."

She waved her torch round her head till it was all ablaze and then flung it down. It fell on that great mass in the middle of the lake. The mass turned slowly over, showing shaggy hair matted with slime. The smell of burning hair came up to us and with it a deep groan that seemed to shake the cave.

We fled in panic. I must indeed ascribe it to chance and to no courage of my own that I kept my grip of the torch. We did not even pause to look at the chalk marks we had made for our guidance, and in consequence found ourselves lost for a while in the labyrinth of passages at the entrance to the cave. At last we found the way out and made our way to the forest. There we spent the remainder of the night, wakeful and talking of the wonders we had seen. It was the last night that we spent together.

The sun had scarcely risen when I saw a few feet away from us a little smoke flickering over the powdered soil.

"What is that?" I asked.

"That is the end," said Dream. "We shall die together."

Rapidly the smoke, which did not rise and disperse, became more opaque, vibrating until it took solid shape. Before us leered the misshapen head and bright beady eyes of the Professor.

His right hand covered with a rubber glove slipped out of the boot and drew forth the death-rod.

"The stranger dies first," he said, and pointed the rod at me. Dream clung to me. I felt a sensation as of fire in my throat.

And now comes what seems to me—though it may not so seem to others—the strangest part of my story. Passing through a kind of swoon, I found myself gently rocked as on board a ship. Opening my eyes I saw two men bending over me. One of them held a glass containing brandy to my lips.

"You see?" said a voice triumphantly. "The beggar's alive and I win my bet."

I found afterwards that I was on board the steamship *Hermione* bound from Alexandria to Cardiff with a cargo of cotton seed. I had been found senseless at the bottom of an open boat. I was treated with plenty of rough kindness and brought back to my own country; but over the story which I told them the crew shook their heads gravely.

Since then nothing of import happened to me until I was brought to this great barrack-like place where I now live in fair comfort. There are many doctors here and many guests. Some of the guests, I fear, have an aberration of the intellect, for they say strange things. I am well contented. I have lived my life. But since no one will listen to my marvellous experiences in the island of Thule—or if they listen at all make a jest of them—I have written them down here for the service of another and a wiser generation.

IN A LONDON GARDEN

CHAPTER I

THE RECLAMATION OF THE CAT-WALK: AND THE STORY OF "THE POOL IN THE DESERT"

My London garden is not really mine. I have it for a period of years on conditions arranged between two legal gentlemen, the tenant paying the landlord's cost. Obviously the person who owns the property can better afford to pay those costs than the man who has to hire it. And similarly the man who is lending money on a mortgage can better afford to pay costs than the man who has to borrow it. But the tenant pays, and the borrower pays. It is a principle of the law that the poor man pays. But this reflection, into which bitterness of spirit has led me, has nothing whatever to do with my garden.

I wasted more than a year. The thing looked quite hopeless. I left my garden to the cats, the jobbing gardeners, the caterpillars, and the other pests.

Of these the worst and most dangerous is perhaps the jobbing gardener. As the law stands at present you may kill a caterpillar, but not a jobbing gardener.

Coming on the wrong day—and he never comes on the right day if he can avoid it—he brings with him a mixed scent of beer and lubricating oil. If the weather is wet, he sits in the potting-shed and smokes. If it is fine, he may possibly mow the lawn. He prefers to mow part of it and then to get on with something else, leaving it like a man with one side of his face shaved. He takes no sort of interest in the garden, and candidly there is no reason why he should take any interest. He only sees the place for a few hours every week, and he would not see it then if he were not paid for it. He has untruthful testimonials, very dirty and decomposed, in his coat pocket, and he is aggrieved when you sack him. This is quite reasonable. A jobbing gardener who attends to the gardens of A, B, and C naturally steals something from A's garden to sell to B, something from B's garden to sell to C, and something from C's garden to sell to A, and thereout sucks he no small advantage. When he gets the sack there is nothing left for him but to steal your secators. He never forgets to do that. I will not say that even in my regenerate condition I never employ a jobbing gardener. There are days when it seems a fine, manly, and primitive thing to do a piece of digging or to mow the lawn. There are more days when such operations seem rather in the light of a nuisance. One would always sooner direct than perform. But the jobbing gardeners who come to me now are under supervision, and are compelled to do things that they hate most in the world—such as putting away their tools when they have finished with them.

I am not particularly fond of the expert and regular gardener either. Generally he has the luck to be a Scotchman and is a man of few words and great knowledge. But his knowledge is always better than his taste, and he debases an art into a science. His ideals would not fit a London garden, and his feeling for colour is often wrong and poisonous.

The horticulturist-and-florist debases a science into a commerce. I have found him useful and shall continue to do so. He saves me trouble. I will deal with him, but I absolutely refuse to admire him.

The amateur gardener would be pleasant if you could cut out his conceit, but it is ineradicable. He comes into my garden and points out my principal mistakes and tells me of the much better things which he has in his garden.

I myself am not a gardener at all. I admit it. I should imagine that there is no man in Great Britain and her Dependencies who knows as little about gardening as I do. But that is not the sole reason why I write about my London garden. We can distinguish between the dog lover and the dog fancier. In the same way we may distinguish between the garden lover and the gardener. It is an important distinction.

The garden in London makes you love it, and it also breaks your heart. It has therefore all the charm of woman. I am not going to believe that any garden in the heart of the country, where everything is green and easy, can give the same pleasure as my half-acre reclaimed among the chimney-pots. It has its limitations, of course, but so have I. So have all human beings. One does not ask a beautiful woman to be clever. One does not expect a clever woman to be beautiful. One does not even hope that an aggressively good woman will be either. Similarly one does not ask the London garden for fruit and vegetables. All that one may really require is shade and flowers. Even that is something, when you remember how very few flowers will grow in shade.

Some blackguard who was allowed to use this garden before it fell to my lot planted rhubarb in a part of it. Most of the rhubarb has now gone, and the rest is going (as the politicians used to say), contrary, I believe, to the terms of my lease. But my landlord is more sympathetic than her solicitors. (The word "landlady" is not to be used. It gives totally wrong associations.) I have also a currant bush, and this shall remain. Its green does not displease me. It produces few currants and I never get or try to get any of them; but birds that are kept as busy with the slugs and caterpillars as the birds in my garden are, deserve an occasional change of diet. I have a few old apple trees and pear trees, but I think I regard them chiefly for their blossom, though these last two years they have taken heart from the enrichment of the soil and have been covered with fruit. You will find parsley and mint in a secluded border, but these represent rather the ornament of nutrition than nutrition itself.

As a rule parsley in London is terribly over-worked. In the refreshment-room at a London terminus late at night I have seen a barmaid collect the sprigs of wilted parsley from the tired sandwiches and sad hard eggs, and put it all in a teacup with a little water. It was heart-breaking to think that that parsley would have to go to work again the next day. But also it presented the barmaid in a new light. It was so foreign to her abnormal stateliness and her unnatural gaiety. It tempted one to believe that after all she was human.

Sitting here in the shade on a hot summer day, with an Austrian brier in full bloom within a few yards of me, I wonder why on earth I ever neglected this garden.

In the first place it had been neglected before. I think for some two years previously a jobbing gardener had called one day every week on purpose to neglect it. Therefore it seemed hopeless to do anything. In the second place it was too rectilineal. It was an exact rectangle, surrounded by straight paths and bisected by one straight path. In the third place I bought a book about gardening for amateurs and it frightened me. It began just about the point where I shall leave off if I live to be a hundred years old.

And then, neglected though it was, the garden made its appeal to me. All round it are tall trees—elm, and chestnut, and wild cherry, and plane, and sycamore. It offered me grateful shade on a hot afternoon, and I had done nothing to deserve it. In the springtime there were mauve blossoms on the lilac, and golden trails on the laburnum, that I had never earned. Later, tall hollyhocks, lavish sunflowers, crowded Michaelmas daisies, added their reproach. I became uneasy. I went out and bought things, such as bast, and fertiliser, and green stakes. I began to wander about the garden, thinking what could be done with it. By the next summer the garden had got a fair hold of me. A man who can learn something fresh is not old, wherefore I am not old, but it surprises me that one of my youth should have learned so amazingly little about a garden in the time.

I began to see encouraging factors. I had not to think about fruit and vegetables. I had not to think about a greenhouse, because the garden has no greenhouse. It has not even got a frame. I shall buy one next year, or possibly the year after. London is simply crawling with florists, and for a few shillings you can buy things all ready to put in. The shilling that goes to the taxicab driver is gone for ever—sacrificed to a fit of laziness. The shilling that buys six sweet-williams provides pleasure for many weeks. The sweet-william is, I believe, a two-year thing, or as the sacred jargon of the gardener puts it, a biennial. You start it one year and it flowers the next. It may be a mean and cowardly thing to do to let the florist do the first year's work on it, and buy it when it is ready to flower that season, but I do it, and I shall continue to do it. I shall continue to do everything that I can think of that will save me trouble in my garden without injuring the garden. But the Iceland poppies are from seed that I myself sowed. I have sown blood-red wallflowers and Canterbury bells to flower next year. One can be lazy without being wholly bad.

Things which looked hopeless at first sight proved better on further consideration. There was the lawn, for instance. The jobbing gardener turned up his nose at the lawn. It slopes. It slopes in several different directions simultaneously.

"There's only one thing to be done with that," said the jobber, "and the sooner you make up your mind to it the better. That all wants to be taken up, levelled, and relaid. It'll cost a bit of money, but it'll never be satisfactory till it's done."

He produced figures and they frightened me. The lawn still slopes deviously, and every day that I see it I am thankful for it. Nobody can possibly play lawn-tennis on it. I hate white rectilineal lines on grass almost more than I hate underdone mutton or "The Lost Chord". Therefore it is a perpetual joy to me that my lawn slopes.

I asked the jobbing gardener what the roses were, planted in odd corners of the lawn.

"Roses!" he said scornfully. "They ain't roses. It's just some common sort of brier. What anybody put it there for, I don't know. It has never flowered for the last three years, and never will flower, and if it did, you wouldn't like it."

Those despised briers are all covered with flower at the present moment, and I like them very much. They are not gardeners' roses, but they are nicer to look at than the Putney bus.

Are there any plantains in my lawn? There are. There is also more grass than there used to be. You can do a lot of things with plantains. If you turn guinea-pigs loose on your lawn, so one newspaper informs me, they will eat the plantains and leave the grass. But I have not got any guinea-pigs, and I am not going to provide a manly but barbarous sport for the cats of the neighbourhood by buying guinea-pigs. Another method is to cut off the head of the plantain and apply lawn-sand. I shall very likely do that one day when there is nothing in the garden which wants doing more, and if I happen to feel like it. A part of a summer day you must work in a London garden, but it is equally true that for another part of the summer day you must just sit and enjoy it. Otherwise you sacrifice the end to the means.

"As for that old box tree," said my jobbing Jeremiah, "it never ought to have been put there at all, right on the edge of a bed. If you take my advice you will have it out. Of course, if it had been properly trimmed and looked after, that might have been made into a peacock, but it would take you years to get it into shape now. You can't grow anything under it, and it's no good trying."

I am glad the old box tree is not a peacock. It has grown the way it wanted to grow, and it suits it. It is perfectly true that nothing will grow under it, and therefore I have not tried to grow anything under it. I found me a handy man and sent him out to buy me a hundred bricks, what time I marked out under the box tree a place where one might sit—a place dry to the feet after the rain. I sent him for red bricks, and he came back with white, because the red bricks were (a) too expensive, and (b) too soft. But the white bricks have done very well with some old bricks mixed in with them, and soon lost their aggressiveness. So underneath my box tree is an L-shaped pavement of bricks, with room for a seat and a table.

People look at it and sniff. It is too unusual. Then they go away and buy bricks. It is astonishing, by the way, how very few bricks there are in a hundred. What I mean, of course, is what a very small pavement they make.

I made another seat under the big scarlet thorn, but this is more ambitious. I got me broken pavement stones—not very easy to get nowadays—and paved a semicircle. On that I put a semicircular seat with a back to it. Irreverent people have compared it *(a)* to a pew, and *(b)* to a loose-box; but it is a pleasant place to sit in in the evening, and just catches the last of the sunlight. After that I dealt firmly with myself, and said that I could not be always making seats.

I began to see ways by which I might make the garden a little less rectilineal. I need hardly say that I wanted a pergola, because of course everybody wants a pergola. The best house-agents say that a riverside cottage lets better if it has a pergola and no dining-room than if it has a dining-room and no pergola. My pergola is built of rustic wood creosoted, which costs very little. It forms a big semicircle with a short tail projecting from the middle of the curve. On it I grow ramblers and glory-roses. I told an expert with some pride what I had done.

"Yes," said the expert sadly and thoughtfully, "almost any rose does well in London, except the Gloire-de-Dijon."

My glory-roses look all right at present, but he is probably correct. When you do a work and do not know how to do it, you are handicapped. Almost the first thing I did in the way of gardening was to put in some gaillardias, which I had bought in a box. Three of them died. It takes a good deal to kill a gaillardia. Things that I plant now do not die. I am certainly getting on. I shall soon be able to say Gloire-de-Dijon when I mean glory-rose.

Perfection is not for me. But there are some pleasant halting-places this side of it. I consult that book for amateur gardeners at intervals, principally because it is such a delight to be able to skip the long chapter about sea-kale. I still struggle, and tell myself frequently that I shall continue to struggle. But, as I have said, there are pleasant halting-places this side of perfection, and I have a great tendency to get out at the next station.

When that tendency comes over me I try to remember the smallness of my garden. In a small garden you may cut the caterpillar nests off the scarlet thorn, and burn them to ashes so that no spark of life remains. You feel sure that not one caterpillar is left in the garden. You may then get to work and pick caterpillars off the rose trees. You may hunt the ubiquitous green fly. You may weed properly with a small fork, instead of perfunctorily with a hoe, after the manner of the jobbing gardener. In time of drought you can water everything. In a small garden much is possible.

It is not exactly a garden yet, of course. The author of that book for amateurs would drop dead from shock if he saw it. But it is more like a garden than the cankered cat-walk it once was.

By the way, speaking of a garden in London, you may possibly have heard the story of

THE POOL IN THE DESERT

There was once a desert. Now I come to think of it, there still is.

Across the desert, mounted on three camels, came the millionaire, the artist, and the analyst. During the day their diet had consisted principally of biscuits and sand. With this they had drunk as much dry sherry as happened to be left in the millionaire's gold flask with the diamond monogram on it. Therefore at first sight they were glad when they saw the pool, and dismounted hurriedly from their camels. But self-respect, which is a splendid quality, came to their rescue. It was the millionaire who spoke first.

"I don't call that a pool at all. I have a lake in the park at my country-place at least four times the size of that. It is a wretched skimpy little business not worth our attention. Now if we had come to the cataract of Niagara, that really would have been of some interest."

Even as he spoke, the analyst had produced from his saddle-bags test tubes, and litmus paper, and a spirit-lamp, and all manner of mixed chemicals, and was busily engaged on a sample of the water which he had taken.

It was the artist who spoke next.

"Water demands green surroundings. To put a pool in a desert is to put it in a wrong setting altogether. Here we have one stunted and miserable palm tree, and no other vegetation. There is really nothing at all here that I should care to paint."

The analyst was now ready with his results.

"This is precisely what I feared. There can be no doubt whatever that this pool suffers from organic pollution. I do not say that it exists to such an extent as to be dangerous to life, but there is a very distinct trace. I will show you the figures in my analysis."

He did so. I have forgotten the figures. But that does not matter, because if I told you them, you also would forget them.

And then for a while these three good men sat and looked at one another.

"I believe I am dying of thirst," said the millionaire.

"So am I," said the artist.

"There is no known form of liquid that I would not at this moment gladly drink," said the analyst.

So after all they turned their attention to the pool.

But in the meantime the three camels—poor dumb beasts who knew no better—had drunk up the whole of that pool, and had gone on their way rejoicing.

CHAPTER II

OMISSIONS: AND THE STORY OF "THE GIRL WHO WENT BACK"

There are smuts in London.

There is also a tradition about the smuts in London, and it may be as well to differentiate the facts and the tradition. According to tradition, everywhere within a six-mile radius from Charing Cross smuts fall heavily and continuously. Nothing will grow. No green things can exist. A sheet of paper exposed to the open air becomes black in three seconds, and a thick layer of carbon covers everything. There are many people who believe this. I was told so only the other night by a beautiful lady to whom I had inadvertently jabbered about my garden. By the way, she was wearing a white dress. Why?

The fact is that there are as many smuts as one can reasonably want—and perhaps a few more—in the city and in Mayfair. There are not so many as there used to be, because there is less smoke. Electricity does not smoke. Up in St John's Wood and Hampstead the smuts are very much diminished. Probably if I climbed one of my trees I should find my hands black. But I am not a boy nor a gorilla, that I should do this thing. I read or write in the garden, and I find that no smut settles on the white page. I dine under the tall trees, and the white cloth remains unpolluted. I may possibly get an elm-seed in my soup, but that is another matter. (Can anyone tell me, by the way, why the elm produces such an amazing lot of seeds and sows them broadcast, with a preference for places where they can never by any possibility germinate?) This is all quite contrary to tradition, but it happens to be the truth.

There is a good time coming—the time when smoke will be eliminated. The London garden will doubtless be an easier and cleaner matter then. But meanwhile the London garden is not impossible. The evergreens are distinctly shop-soiled after the winter; but with the summer comes the fresh green, and in the summer London provides us with less smoke from fewer fires. Beautiful white dresses must be washed or cleaned, and after all the garden has its hose and its rain-showers.

The tradition is inept as it stands, but it has a basis of truth. There is very much that must be omitted in the London garden. There are flowers that never come to town. Speaking generally, bulbs will do less work here than they will in the country. After the first year the tulips get tired. But as a compensation for the many things which one must omit, come the many other things which one may omit.

The liberty of the subject is too much circumscribed, but I believe that there is no law in this country which compels a man to grow the Jacoby geranium. This does not seem to be generally understood. Look at the window-boxes of London, and look at the gardens. Mayfair as a rule is ambitious and kills quite pretty things in its window-boxes; but elsewhere all too frequently one finds the Jacoby geranium and the edging of blue lobelia. I think that people get these things and grow them just exactly as they pay their dog licence—not because they want to do it but because they feel they must. There is probably an organised conspiracy between florists and jobbing gardeners to promote Jacobys. "You will be wanting some geraniums," says the florist decisively, and you are hypnotised into believing it. "What could we have in that bed?" you ask the jobbing gardener. "A few Jacobys," he says, with the air of a man who has had a bright idea. If he does not edge them with blue lobelia, he edges them with some yellow stuff which I think he calls pyrethrum. One has only to smell it once never to try it again. At the same time there are some super-cultured people who carry the hatred of the geranium to an unreasonable extent. There is a white one which does not make me ill, and a pink one which is not too hideous. But as it happens, the only geranium in my garden is the one which is grown solely for the scent of its leaves. One year where geraniums might have been I had blue-violet verbenas, sweet-scented and just as easy to grow. I was told to hairpin them to the ground, but out of obstinacy I grew them upright. They did not seem to mind. I have no rage against the blue lobelia, if it is put in a safe place where its colour can do no harm. I do not know why the white lobelia has so much less popularity. One is not bound to grow it as an edging. Now I come to think of it, I believe I hate all edgings.

I am not very fond of those flowers which are distinctively villa flowers. I do not think there is any man alive who could sell me a yellow calceolaria or persuade me to find room for it in my garden. The fuschia too is rather a self-conscious and ostentatious thing, though I admit the tree-fuschia. To these I prefer musk, and mignonette, and heliotrope. They flourish in a wet summer, and I wish I did. Lilies and carnations of course one must have, and London permits it. London pride is common enough, but I like it and grow it. It is a generous thing that asks little and gives much. If only its graceful flower were expensive, it would be greatly admired. The white and yellow marguerites are of no dazzling rarity, but I welcome them. Hosts of the old-fashioned perennials are desirable and possible, though there are some of them that need to be watched. The sunflower, for instance, is distinctly greedy and would take the whole garden if it could get it.

If a general principle of omission and selection for a London garden could be formulated, it would probably run as follows—choose cottage-garden things and avoid villa-garden things. In this way you will get all that is simple and sweet-scented and easy of cultivation, and nothing which is formal and perky. There are men who at present do earn large salaries by making gardens perky. The pity of it!

I have myself seen a long bed covered with things of different coloured foliage in geometrical patterns. "You may see as good Sights, many times, in Tarts." Thank you, my Lord Verulam, for those words. Looking at such a bed one did not see the flowers only. The eye of imagination lingered on all that must have conduced to its preparation—all the pegs, and string, and perspiration, and misplaced cleverness. A garden may easily be over-educated, and that which is good in itself may suffer from improvement.

And that reminds me. You do not, perhaps, know the story of

THE GIRL WHO WENT BACK

There was once a girl whose name was Rose, and she was rather pretty and rather clever. She was not very pretty or very clever, but everybody said she was very sweet. She had great advantages. Her papa was a wise man. Her mamma—well, her mamma had the best intentions and was troubled with ambition. But they both loved Rose.

The ambitious mamma said to the wise papa: "Rose is now seventeen years old. She has faults which must be eradicated. She has good qualities which must be enhanced. The last year of her education must be peculiarly strenuous."

"As how?" said the wise papa.

"Well, I do not quite like the way she speaks. Her voice is pleasant in quality, and you can generally understand her; but she slurs her words and she is just a little weak on the letter 'r'. She must be made to pay far more attention to her personal appearance. Her waist is not as small as it might be; and her complexion—but these are not things which you will require to understand. She must learn German thoroughly. A smattering is no use. She must not be allowed to have her own way about the violin. Arithmetic is a very weak point with her. Are you attending?"

The wise papa opened his eyes, and said that he had heard every word, and that she was quite certain to be right, and that he would leave it to her.

Rose had no ambition and no wisdom. She liked play. She liked real music. She liked dancing. But as she was quite good, she did what she was told. Many tutors came about her, and she worked early and late. Her mother confided to her those secrets which should add to her beauty.

The elocution master was quite pleased with her. She learned to ar-tic-u-late her words and to speak dis-tinct-ly. She pronounced every "r" as if it had been a coffee-mill. It was a treat to listen to her.

Her proficiency in foreign languages was really remarkable.

Her music teacher said that she had improved enormously in technique and in taste. Her playing on the violin was a mixture of gymnastics and conjuring tricks. She learned to speak slightingly of melody. She understood advanced orchestration, and pronounced Tschaikowsky correctly. She occasionally annoyed people by giving Chopin the Russian pronunciation.

Her waist became smaller. You might have thought that her long hours of study would have made her pale, but there was always a delicate blush on either cheek-bone, except when she had just washed her face. Her hair became a work of art. It was marvellously arranged.

The college of domestic-training found Rose its most apt pupil. She could cook. She could housekeep. Her arithmetic was unfailing. She could detect at once the mistake in the tradesman's account, and she could get the right note of asperity into her voice in speaking to him about it. "Is it not rather an extraordinary coincidence that these frequent errors are always in your own favour?" This was obviously the kind of woman that a sensible man would be glad to marry. She was a highly developed helpmeet.

The ambitious mamma saw that Rose had improved out of all knowledge. She became proud of her. She now waited for Rose to make an exceptionally brilliant match. She continued to wait, for something had changed in Rose. People said she was very accomplished and very beautiful, but nobody said she was rather sweet. The boys who had played with her and danced with her did not seem to require her any more; they shivered with fear in her splendid presence.

We should all improve ourselves, and try to do our best—this is the accepted view and there is no need to dispute it—but concentration on one's own self, even with the highest possible motive, is poison. And Rose had drunk of that poison.

And then the ambitious mamma died; and there were some people who thought that she was better dead. But Rose was overcome with grief. It was not until six weeks later that, standing before the cheval-glass, she noticed how very well she looked in black. She worked harder than ever at the task of self-improvement, until her health broke down. Then two things happened simultaneously. She was ordered into the country, and her papa went to take up an important post in Paris.

Rose lived now in a cottage up on a hill with a refined and elderly lady-companion. Beyond the garden of the cottage was common-land. Here the bracken grew waist-high, and you might see as many foxgloves in ten minutes as you would find in London in ten years. Sheep roamed among the bracken. The difference between the face of the lady-companion and the face of one of those sheep was hardly noticeable; they also had similarities in disposition.

When the lady-companion slept—and she was a perfectly grand sleeper—Rose wandered all the afternoon about the common. She was not improving herself any longer, because that was held to be bad for her health. She worried because she felt that she had lost the love of people. The longer she lived in the country, the more she wanted to be loved. She even put tentative questions to the lady-companion, to find out how it was that she was not loved. But these tentative questions were of no use, because the lady-companion maintained that Rose was loved very much indeed, being under the impression that this was the kind of thing that she was paid to say. She was a conscientious woman.

And then one night Rose had a dream. In her dream she heard a loud knocking at the cottage door, and she herself went to see who was there.

There stood a very ugly old pedlar with a leer on his face, and a pack on his back. He swung his pack round and took off the piece of American cloth from the top of it.

"And what can I sell you to-day, my pretty lady?" he asked.

"Nothing, thank you," said Rose.

"Don't say that," said the pedlar. "You have dealt with me before, you know."

"Never," said Rose. "You are mistaken."

"Yes, you did," said the ugly old man stoutly. "You bought a packet of Amoricide, and those that deal with me once must deal with me again."

"What is Amoricide?" asked Rose, who began to have a feeling that after all she did recognise the pedlar's face.

"Well, well," said the pedlar, "that's telling. I don't mind owning that there is a lot of the Air of Superiority in it, and there are other things. You have no complaint to make about it, have you? It does its work all right. I guarantee that it will exterminate love absolutely. It is death to love. Have you not found it so?"

"I have found," said Rose, "that it has destroyed the love of others for me, but not the love of me for others."

The old man chuckled. "That's it. That's right. That's why the people who deal with me once must deal with me again. You must have one more little packet."

"This time I want to know what is in it."

The pedlar began to look uneasy. "Don't ask too many questions. We call it Taedium Vitae. It is a splendid thing."

Rose was highly educated, and she told him that Taedium Vitae meant life-weariness, and that she would like to know how it acted.

"You go down the hill," said the old man absent-mindedly, as if he were speaking to himself, "and then, of course, you come to the pine wood."

Rose nodded. "Yes, I know it. Through the wood is the short cut if you are going to the station. The stile is rather awkward to climb over."

"You can manage it all right. You have done it before. And you know the dark pool under the trees?"

Rose nodded. This time she did not speak.

"That's another short cut," said the old man with a chuckle. "It's soon over. The sensation of drowning is said to be quite pleasant. Then there is no more trouble—no more worrying because you have lost love, and because life has lost its savour."

Rose was rather frightened. "When do I pay you?" she asked in a husky whisper.

"That's all right," said the old man ingratiatingly. "You don't pay me till afterwards. We give credit."

"Afterwards?"

"After the pool. Come, you will take this packet."

"I will not," said Rose with sudden determination, and shut the door in the old man's ugly face. He kept on knocking.

Then she knew that it was only the knocking of the maid who brought her one cup of China tea, one piece of thin bread-and-butter, one large can of hot water, and the news that it was a fine morning.

After that there was a change in Rose. Some of the change was very subtle. Some of it was quite obvious. Even a lady-companion with the mind of a sheep can detect a change in personal appearance. She did detect it, and she spoke about it with discretion.

Rose answered: "Yes, two inches bigger. I don't wear them at all now. Suppose I shall have to when I go back to town. And I find I simply cannot stand the other stuff. If I've got brown, that is because God's sun meant me to be brown."

"The merest touch would——"

Rose was good-humoured, but obstinate.

And in time she went back to town. She had lost the habit of thinking about herself or of asking why people did not love her. She gave them the music that they wanted, and not the music that she knew they ought to have wanted. She became very simple and friendly. The tone of her voice softened, and the "r" sound no longer buzzed properly. She had gone back. And when she was not thinking about it at all, people began to love her.

One man particularly. And this was fortunate for Rose.

Papa, who was a director of Kekshose & Cie—they make such big motor-cars that nobody ever dares to let them do as much as they will, and hardly anybody can afford to buy them—came back for the wedding.

I was just going to say, when that foolish story interrupted me, that Cardinal Newman wrote a book called "Apologia pro vita sua." I mention it not as a discovery but as a reminder. I believe that almost every imaginative author writes an *Apologia pro vita sua*, though under a different title and in a different guise. I could name one author (and so, of course, could you) who has written several such apologiæ. If I have never done it myself, it is because I am not of the heroic type which undertakes lost causes. But I am not quite sure that I am not writing an *Apologia pro horto meo*. There is a serpent in every Eden, and its name is Pride. If my half-acre of cat-walk can claim to be a remote descendant of Eden, the serpent exists there too. I point out the good things in the garden. I cover up the defects, or—which is even worse—I make elaborate explanations to prove that they are not defects at all. I cannot expect anybody to like my garden as much as I do, but I want them to respect it. Jokes about it always seem to me to be in bad taste. A very good amateur gardener once came into my garden and mentioned just a few of the things that he noticed. He did it in the kindliest way. He taught me quite a good deal, and I hope he will never know how near I came to beating him on the head with the business end of a large rake.

I think that what I have said about omission is true. Everybody who loves art loves omission. I should like, for instance, if I could, to write in the fewest words that lucidity requires. It has given me pleasure to omit certain things from my garden.

But all the same—and I may as well confess it—fewer things would be omitted from my garden if it were larger and in the heart of the country, and if I had somebody to help me, and if by chance I happened to know something about it.

CHAPTER III

ROSES: AND THE STORY OF "THE BLESSED ARTIST"

The terminology of the botanist is a standard joke, but as a matter of fact, the botanist blunders into a good thing sometimes. It was rather a fine idea to have in plants an order of those that bear the cross—cruciferæ. The turnip and sea-kale are among those whose petals make the sign, but it need not shock us. Is there not loveliness in the flower of the potato, and poetry in the foliage of the asparagus? On the whole, I think the botanist makes me less angry than the horticulturist.

Why, for instance, are so many roses named after abominable horticulturists or their wearisome female relatives? How can you call a rose Frau Karl Druschki? I always call that great white rose Mabel, because it reminds me of a large, lymphatic, handsome girl, who was entirely without charm. Scent in a flower is charm in a woman. Frau Karl Druschki has no scent. Hugh Dickson has nothing wrong with it but its name. Fancy calling a beautiful apricot-tinted rose William Allen Richardson! Its godfathers and godmothers in its baptism showed a small sense of humour. Besides, its name is quite obviously Doris. It is permissible to call a pink rambler Dorothy, but why add the unspeakable surname Perkins? Why should a red rose be named after a duke? It is insufferable, snobbish, and inept. No rose should be named after any man, and should never bear more than the first name of a woman. Niphetos is a possible name; it is the most sentimental of the white roses. But almost all roses have their counterparts in women. There is, for instance, in my garden a pink, useful, knobbly dumpling of a rose. I have not the faintest idea what the horticulturist would call it, but no one can see it without knowing that its real name is Kate.

I think the roses that I love best are those of the deepest and darkest crimson. They have velvety skins and the most perfect fragrance. It is part of the perversity of the thing that they should be so difficult to manage. You feed them and tend them, and they give you scanty and imperfect bloom, or they die, and the intelligent inquest results in an open verdict. When that happens, the only consolation is to find somebody else who has had the same trouble with the same rose. I have not ventured to ask one of them to put up with a London garden as yet, but I fancy one is coming to stay with me next year. Perversity haunts the garden, and the dock always grows as near as possible to some plant that you value. "Now then," says the dock, "if you dig me up, you'll have to pay for it." But especially does perversity attach itself to roses. What have I done for the perennial lupins? Nothing. And they have given me numberless spikes of incomparable loveliness. What have I done for the Canterbury bells? Nothing. And they also seem to like it. But I did a good deal for that particular rose which I call Mabel, and then there was a late spring frost. It was no fault of mine. I was not even there when it was done. I was in bed at the time. But it annoyed Mabel. She seemed unable to forget it. Why must those loathsome and parthenogenetic green flies devour the tender roses? There is still a certain amount of rhubarb in the garden, and they are welcome to it. I would very much rather they ate it than that I should eat it myself. But the green flies will not look at it. They cling to the rose and suck its life out. Then, out of sheer devilry, they grow wings and migrate to some other rose tree.

The queen demands homage, and the rose has received it to the extent of countless volumes written by wise gardeners who have studied her specially. Their learning appals. They almost deter the poor blunderer in London from ever trying to grow a rose or to talk about one. A little knowledge may be a dangerous thing, but the expert runs his risks also. I was taken through a most beautiful rose-garden once, and I dared to admire one particular bed. "Yes," said the owner of the garden almost apologetically, "it's quite one of the old sorts." And then I was taken to other beds in which was the very last word in roses—kinds that had only been produced within the last year or so—and here the owner showed more enthusiasm. Has it come to this then—that fashion is to stray from the milliner's shop and find a place in the garden?

From motives of humanity I refrain from bringing out once more certain over-worked quotations from Herrick and Omar; but in truth the poets, like the scientific gardeners, have not spared writing materials where roses were in question. They are ecstatic about the colour and fragrance, and generally sentimental about the thorns, and never by any chance allude to the culture. There is something feminine about poets. They like the result, but they ignore the process, just as a woman eats a lamb cutlet, but does not want you to talk about the slaughter-house. Perhaps it is not to be expected that poets should mention the food of the roses, and yet I hate a shirker of facts. I am not sure that there is not something of poetry in the plain truth that in nature's impartial chemistry there is only one step from muck to glory.

And now, if you are tired of uninformative talk about roses, I will tell you the story of

THE BLESSED ARTIST

There was once an artist who lived in a great town. He was painting a picture, and he took a great deal of trouble to make it as difficult for himself as possible. He tried for effects of lighting that needed miracles. In his work he sought and worshipped difficulties. In the garden beyond the studio he found plenty of difficulty without seeking for it. But this was difficulty of a kind that maddened him. He wanted a garden, but he did not want to make a garden. So he employed a man one day a week, and was profoundly dissatisfied.

One afternoon he had a dream. He dreamed that an angel came into his room —a beautiful angel of the accepted Doré Gallery type. The angel had a pleasant voice and said pleasant things to him.

"You have lived well," said the angel, "and you have worked well. You have earned for yourself the blessedness that belonged to the Garden of Eden. That blessedness shall fall upon your garden. Go and look at it."

So the artist went out on to his lawn and was quite surprised. It was of one beautiful tint of fresh green all over, with never a brown spot. There had been many daisies on that lawn, but they had all gone now. It had suffered from moss, but the moss had vanished. It had been superficially irregular, but it was now level. The perfect grass was just three-quarters of an inch in height, and no tall bents stuck up anywhere. He went to look at his roses. He remembered them as they had formerly been—spindly bushes which he had forgotten to prune, and that bore leaves only at the extreme end of their branches. They had changed to compact bushes that were green all over and flowered like an illustration in a seedsman's catalogue. Caterpillars had played havoc with them aforetime, but now he could find no caterpillar and no trace of the caterpillar's work. He went on to his two apple trees. They had borne no blossom that year that he could remember, and the white tufts of American blight had bedecked their trunks. The American blight was all gone now. The blossom had set, and the fruit was swelling, and each tree would bear exactly the right number of apples, neither more nor less. The carnations were very large, numerous, and fragrant. The madonna lilies promised well. There was no weed to be seen anywhere, and the paths had been newly gravelled with the red gravel which he had always wanted, and never been able to get. The very quality of the soil had changed, and was now dark and rich. It was worth while to work in such a garden as this; he took his coat off and went into the potting-shed to get his tools.

And then he realised his blessedness. There was absolutely nothing for him to do in the garden. It was all quite good. The drought had not brought down the leaves nor cracked the surface. The strong winds had not dishevelled and laid low the sunflowers. He noticed, moreover, that things were tied up now with green bast to green sticks. He had always wanted green bast and green sticks, but had used the other kind because it was the only kind that the man round the corner sold.

He put on his coat and stretched himself on a deck-chair on the lawn in the evening sunlight in a great state of contentment. When it grew dusk, from the shrubbery at the end of the garden came beyond mistake the voice of the nightingale. He had always wanted nightingales, but so far he had put up with imitative blackbirds. Blessedness had come to him indeed.

He lit a cigarette and reflected how he would show his garden to Smith, and how much Smith would be annoyed about it. Smith had a garden of his own, and was a toilsome amateur with a certain amount of knowledge. Smith would undoubtedly be green with jealousy. He would ask Smith to luncheon, and afterwards they would have coffee in the garden. He would carefully abstain from calling Smith's attention to anything; but he would watch him, as he slowly drank it all in and meditated suicide.

On the day that Smith was to come to luncheon, the blessed artist rose early in order that he might mow the lawn before breakfast. But when he went out, he found that it did not require to be mown. The grass grew to just the right height and then stopped. At luncheon Smith was inflated with pride, and talked freely about begonias. He mentioned other things which he had in his garden—things that that artist ought to come and see. The artist sat quite meekly, and was very polite until luncheon was over. Then he said: "I think we might have coffee in the garden, Smith, if you call that backyard of mine a garden."

"Ah," said Smith, "you should give a little more time and attention to it."

Then they passed out into the garden, and Smith was struck dumb. At last he said: "How do you manage to get those fine dark wallflowers in full bloom at the end of June?"

"Takes a bit of management," said the blessed artist complacently.

Smith began to walk round the garden. He admired exceedingly. The confession that he had got nothing like that escaped him frequently; and when he had seen it all, he pulled from one pocket an old envelope and from another a short stubb of a pencil.

"Look here," he said, "you might just give me the name of the chap who does your garden for you."

"The angels do my garden for me," said the blessed artist.

"Oh, all right," said Smith, "if you don't want to tell me, you needn't."

And he put back the old envelope and the pencil in their respective pockets, and he went away in a very bad temper. But this incident reminded the blessed artist to countermand the jobbing gardener—a man of intemperate habits and quite unfit to collaborate with angels.

The next day the artist went into his garden and enjoyed it extremely.

The day after he enjoyed it less.

The day after that he began to be dissatisfied. Dissatisfaction began to settle like a cloud upon him. He wondered why. It came to him slowly that he felt like a man who had stolen the Victoria Cross and was wearing it ostentatiously. He was exhibiting a perfection for which he had never worked; and there was no savour in it.

"Better," he cried, "imperfection towards which one has contributed something. Better even the sickly wilderness that this garden once was."

The sound of his own voice woke him.

He found that he was sitting in a deck-chair on the lawn. It was a decayed chair, having been left out in many rains. The lawn was just as bad as ever it had been. He could almost hear the caterpillars crunching up the surrounding vegetation. One glance showed him that his rose trees were still a shame and a reproach. And down the steps from the house came his old friend Smith, smiling and rubicund.

"Been asleep in this rotten old garden of yours?" he said. "It looks to me as if you would have done better if you had been working in it."

"I am inclined to think so," said the artist.

As a rule it is easier to do much work than little. The man who is underworked rarely does the little that he has to do thoroughly and punctually. The more leisure one has, the more one desires.

I feel confident that if I had a thousand rose trees, I should be up bright and early in the morning to do for them all that they required. I should study the literature on the subject and become expert. Possibly I should not go so far as some experts, who provide a kind of conical tin hat for each rose bloom to shelter it from the rain. But it would not be slackness which would stay my hand; it would be because I cannot think that the conical tin hat adds greatly to the beauty of the garden.

But I have not got a thousand rose trees. It is none the less essential that I should cut off all the dead blooms. This labour, carried out with no unseemly haste, might possibly occupy me for five minutes.

And how many times have I shirked those five minutes of labour? I am shirking them now. Let me see, where are the scissors?

CHAPTER IV

THE FOUNTAIN: AND THE STORY OF "THE LITTLE DEATH"

I will admit that I very nearly erected a sun-dial in my garden. There was a kind of snobbery about it. So many artistic people have erected sun-dials in their gardens, that I supposed that I should be artistic if I erected a sun-dial in mine. But all the time, somewhere at the back of my head, was the conviction that the thing was rotten. I knew it was rotten some time before I knew the reason why.

Sun-dials are not used nowadays for the purpose of telling the time. It is therefore insincere and affected to put a sun-dial in a modern garden. It is not conscientious. It is like the artificial creation of worm-holes in the spurious-antique furniture. Where the sun-dial already exists in an old garden one may be glad of it, but one may not deliberately put a sun-dial into a new garden.

So I put in a fountain.

The simplest and most satisfactory way to get a fountain in one's garden is to buy one from the fountain shop, make arrangements with the Water Company, and get a real plumber to fix it. This did not appeal to me. There was no adventure about it, it would cost too much, and I knew that I should hate shop-fountains. I therefore designed and made my own fountain, and will now instruct others how they may make one which will be nearly as bad and delightful.

The first step is to find among your acquaintances a family where the baby is grown up. Talk about babies. Ask if the baby had a tin bath with a lid to it, the kind that its things are packed in when it goes to the seaside in the summer. Ask further if that bath is still in existence. If it is, then make the family give you the bath. It is to serve as the reservoir for your fountain and is essential.

You proceed to the second step. In deciding where you would put your fountain, you will remember of course that fountains always look best among big trees with a green background. You now fix the disused bath firmly in the tree twenty feet or so from the ground, in such a position that it is secluded by foliage from the gaze of the curious and impertinent. The chestnut tree seems to have been specially designed by nature for this purpose.

Your third step would be to dig out the basin of the fountain. I chose a spot under the trees mid ferns and laurels. I bought from a stone-yard a cartload of material, half of it broken flat paving-stone and half of it chunks, and I may add incidentally that I paid too much for it. I paved the bottom of the basin with flat stone and concrete, leaving a space for the jet of the fountain to come up in the middle. I used the flat stone also for the border round the margin of the basin. At the back of the fountain I built up the chunks to the height of six feet or so, putting in plenty of earth with them. I have golden and silver ivies climbing over the stones, and I have planted there anything which I thought would grow.

The reservoir being in its place and the basin constructed, the next step is to connect them. This is done by a compo pipe with a surreptitious tap in it.

And after that you fill the bath with the garden hose and turn the tap. As a rule nothing happens the first time, because there is air in the pipe; but you can put the garden syringe to the fine nozzle in which the compo pipe terminates, and draw out the air. My own fountain will play for six hours continuously; and then when no one is looking one must fill up the bath reservoir again.

It is really extraordinary how gardening turns decent, God-fearing men into braggarts. I have said that I did this myself. I did design it. I did direct the work, and to some extent assist in it; but can I fix compo pipes on to holes in baths, or fine nozzles on to compo pipes? Can I fit taps? Can I manipulate stone and concrete? Certainly not.

It is very useful to know a man who can do everything, especially when one gets ambitious in a London garden. The same man who did the plumbing work of the fountain also did the stone work. He built the palace—it were an affectation of modesty to call it a kennel—in which the Pekinese puppy lives when it is not eating the Iceland poppies. He painted the garden seats. He is an expert in the removal of the American blight. He has diagnosed that my wild cherry is bark-bound, and wishes me to let him cut a slit in it, but I dare not. He is wonderful and he is inexpensive.

The public fountain is always placed in an open space. There is a tendency even among quite decent private people to use the fountain as a lawn decoration. I like it better among trees myself; it is more classical. It recalls more lines of Horace. The fountain must never be allowed to play on a dull or cold day. And if you yourself are doing something strenuous in the garden, it is irksome to have the fountain playing while you are working. The fountain belongs to sunlight and repose, and the garden that is not a place of rest is no garden. The purr of the lawn-mower and the tinkle of falling water are the two most soporific sounds in existence. They should be used by the medical profession in the cure of insomnia. I do not know why, but people generally seem to be a little proud of insomnia. They like to tell you how many times in the night they heard the clock strike. One will do almost anything to be interesting, undeterred by failure in it. This, I suppose, it is which drives some to story-writing.

You may have chanced to hear the story of

THE LITTLE DEATH

There was once (but it must have happened a long time ago and in some very distant island) a race of people who never slept. Occasionally they became tired and lay down, but they never closed their eyes and never lost consciousness. They had never heard of sleep. They had never learned it. And in consequence they did a great deal of work, but they died very young. They were quite happy about it of course, because one never misses what one has never had. There may be something quite as sweet as sleep which we ourselves do not miss, only because we do not know about it.

One day a shipwrecked man was cast up on the shore. These were hospitable people, and they took him up to the King's palace and entertained him. And when night came, after he had feasted and drunk, the King said: "And now what pleasure can we offer you? Would you like to hear music, or to see the dancing-girls, or to ride out in the moonlight?"

The man laughed. "None of these things, sir," he said. "The day has been long, and a feeling of weariness overcomes me. I should now like to sleep."

"That is some new game?" asked the King, intelligently.

"Sleep?" said the Princess Melissa. "We do not know that. What is this sleep?"

The man explained it as best he could, and his account was received with the greatest interest. Many questions were put to him.

"I perceive," said the King at last, "that this sleep is really a little death. For the time being you are dead. Take my advice, therefore, O stranger, and give it up. It is an awful risk, thus voluntarily to enter into the place of death. Suppose that one day you find something there that keeps you, and you cannot come back again."

The stranger explained that, so far was this from being the case, that every time when he went to sleep he was more afraid that something would wake him, than that he would never wake at all.

"I fear," said the King, "that this shows that you have not thought about the matter profoundly."

"Possibly not," said the stranger. "But I am as I am constructed. I sleep because I must sleep. Had I but a couch to lie upon, I could be asleep now in five minutes."

"How exciting," said the Princess Melissa.

"May we all see it? May we watch you when you are dead of the little death?"

"Most certainly," said the stranger politely. "I am so tired that I am likely to sleep very soundly, but all the same noise or bright light would wake me again, and that would make me very angry. I must beg, therefore, that when you come to look upon me in my sleep, the light may be subdued and no sound may be made."

And to this condition they agreed.

A room was prepared for the stranger in the palace. It was thickly carpeted, so that no footfall could sound. It had a curtained entrance, that the stranger might not be disturbed by the sound of the door opening and shutting when people entered to see the show. The room was dimly lit by the flame of a small lamp. In five minutes the stranger was asleep.

One by one they entered the room—the King, the Princess, and all the people of the court—to see this new and awful phenomenon of a man who was dead of his own volition and would yet come to life again. Three ladies of the court fainted on leaving the apartment. The King became terribly anxious. "This is a dangerous game," he said, "and must be stopped at once. We do not wish to have the death of this stranger on our conscience. Bring, therefore, bright lights and make a loud noise——"

But here the Princess Melissa intervened. "No," she said; "he is not really dead, for he still breathes. I watched him most carefully and am sure of it. It is an experiment which he has often made. He tells me that he has had this sleep every night of his life."

"Doubtless," said the King, "he wished to make an impression; we are not bound to believe that."

But the King was bound to admit, though he did so grudgingly, that a man who breathed was not a dead man.

All the night through they watched outside the sleeping-chamber, and about the middle of the night they heard a terrific sound.

"That," said the King, "is the cry of his death agony. I know it. I am sure of it. We have done wrong."

As a matter of fact, the sound was the first snore which had ever been heard in that island. It made even the Princess Melissa nervous. But she investigated the phenomenon and reported that no interference seemed to be required. The man was not only breathing, he was breathing more strenuously than he did when he was awake.

Nevertheless a great weight was taken from the King's mind when his guest came back to life again in the morning. It was noted that the man was none the worse for his strange experience. He seemed even better for it. He was more active and alert. His eye was brighter. He was instantly ready to undertake the fatigue of swimming for a long distance in the sea.

That morning, as he conversed with the Princess Melissa, he tried to explain to her something even more strange than sleep—the dreams that come to one in sleep. The two walked alone through the forest together.

"Tell me," said the Princess, "do you think that I also could sleep and have a dream? I know it is bizarre and morbid, but I long passionately and above all things to have this strange experience."

"So far as I can judge," said her companion, "you are constructed precisely as the women of the rest of the world, where sleep is a nightly event. I may be wrong, but I should imagine that if the initial impulse could be given to you, you also would sleep."

The Princess clasped her hands in ecstasy. "How perfectly splendid!" she said. "But then how am I to get the initial impulse?"

"What," asked the man, "is that glow of red amid the yellow in the field yonder?"

"That is where poppies grow among ripening corn. But what have they to do with the initial impulse?"

"They are it," said the stranger; "by means of those poppies I could prepare for you the secret of sleep. But there would be a risk."

"You told me just now that in a dream it seemed to you that you were sitting in a boat with an elephant, drinking tea, and the elephant had on a small white coat with a rose in its buttonhole. That seemed as real to you in the dream as it seems now that you are walking with me on the edge of the forest?"

"Quite as real, absolutely real."

"Then for such a miraculous experience as that, who would not run any risk? Come, we will go and gather poppies."

For the next few days the stranger was shut up in his apartments in the palace, making the sleep-producing drug of which he knew. He had to test it many times, that he might be assured that the Princess ran no risk. And during these days the Princess Melissa gathered dry bracken and carried it to the ruined temple that stood in the heart of the forest. For it was there that she meant to yield to her great adventure.

The man continued to sleep at nights, always before a good audience. For the wonderful story had been bruited abroad, and all the people in the land were eager to see. One night he slept for a charity in which the King was interested. Money was turned away at the doors, and the thing was a great financial success. But one newspaper of the island complained of the morbid character of the exhibition. "We cannot," wrote the editor, "approve that this poor sufferer should be made to earn money by what is doubtless his disease."

The time came at last on a hot afternoon in July. The Princess drank the potion that was given her and lay down on the bed of bracken. The stranger watched by her side.

"It is going to fail. I am not asleep," said the Princess; "I do not see elephants or boats or anything but what is really here."

"Close your eyes," said the stranger; "relax your muscles, breathe regularly, and count every breath you take up to ten. Then begin to count again."

"It is no use," said the Princess wearily.

But in a few minutes she was fast asleep.

The Princess was young. Two years before she had fallen in love with a man whom she could not marry, and the man had fallen in love with her. There had been no scandal, such was the discretion that they used, but there had been material for a scandal. The matter was all over now, for the man in his wisdom had gone away.

When the Princess awoke, she sighed deeply.

"You have slept?" said the man.

"I have."

"You have dreamed?"

"I have."

"Tell me your dream."

"I cannot tell you my dream, but I have been to Paradise."

"Les yeux gris vont au Paradis," quoted the man.

"Now give me more of the poppy juice," said the Princess.

"No," said the man, "I have given you as much as you may take safely in one day."

So the Princess pretended to be meek and obedient, and said it was very well and she would think no more about it, and perhaps now sleep would come to her at nights even if she did not drink the poppy juice. That had broken down the barrier of the garden of sleep, and now she would be able to enter the garden freely when she would.

"Perhaps," said the man.

But when for many nights she tried and could not sleep, she grew rebellious, and going secretly to his apartments she procured the poppy juice he had prepared. With this treasure in her hand, she went back to the temple and stretched herself again on the bed of bracken. She drank the whole of the poppy juice.

"For," she said aloud, "if the little death be so sweet, then—then——"

And here she fell asleep.

For ten successive days I had forgotten to buy the weed-killer; therefore on the tenth day, which was a Wednesday, I went out to weed the gravel paths with my own hands. It is not a pleasant operation. It is, I believe, the thing in gardening that I loathe most.

The faint burble of water led me towards my fountain. It was playing joyously, and some careless person had left beside it a garden-chair and the current issue of *Punch*.

Any man with a sense of duty and a reasonable amount of will-power would have turned off the fountain and got to work.

The sun was shining brightly. The day was warm. I had not seen that number of *Punch*. And I did not turn off the fountain, I turned off the work.

But the next day I remembered to buy weed-killer. The commonest saying of the Spaniard is not duly appreciated in this country, and is especially useful in the summer-time.

CHAPTER V

THE STRUGGLE: AND THE STORY OF "ALFRED SIMPSON"

The garden is peaceful, and this is the more extraordinary because it is really the perpetual scene of the bloodiest warfare, and this warfare is the more acute in a London garden because in London there are more enemies. One has the fight of the gardener against natural conditions, his fight against the enemies of his plants, and the fight of the plants among themselves.

One season there was a prolonged drought and the leaves of the trees fell prematurely. "That's due to the drought," said the experts. The following year the season was very wet, and once more my trees shed their leaves before the time. "What else can you expect after all the rain we've had?" said the experts. And in both seasons the dairymen, who seem to have a touch of the expert about them, raised the price of milk. Perhaps one year I shall find the kind of season which exactly suits my London garden.

To fight the drought I got me a great length of hose, and made the usual arrangements with the Water Board. But once the question of a garden is raised, the Water Board also seems to be infected with the military spirit. I had a printed document from them, which was severe to the point of truculence. They reserve themselves rights. They do not guarantee. They are not responsible. They strictly forbid. With these and similar phrases they teach the man who dares to use a hose what a poor worm he is. They tell me that the hose must not be left unattended. What am I to do with it then? Am I to sit up all night with it and hold its nozzle? A wet season brings home to me the awful injustice of Water Boards. Nobody who can get rain for his garden will use the hard, less satisfactory, but highly valuable products of the Water Board. But in the wet season, as in the dry, the consumer must pay. In strict justice, the amount one pays for the water supply for the hose should in any season be in inverse proportion to the rainfall during that season.

When the drought was here I watered my lawn profusely (and the Water Board need not rage and swell, for I never left the hose unattended for one moment). A little later I walked over the lawn to collect its gratitude, as it were, and I saw hosts of strange and horrid things. They were white, and yellow, and yellowish brown. They had come out of the crevices, and they had crawled. When I thought that for weeks past, this, my garden, had been providing them with sustenance, I was moved to fury. But I did not lose my head. There is a right way and a wrong way of doing everything. There is even a right way of killing slugs.

I have read in books that the gardener takes the slug and crushes it under his heel on the gravel path; a jobbing gardener might possibly do that—jobbing gardeners will do anything. Any man who does that is not fit to have a garden. He is only fit to collect house refuse in an open cart during hot weather.

My own method is simple and refined. I have a large jar filled with a strong solution of salt and water. I have, moreover, a large pair of surgical forceps serrated on the inner edge, price one shilling at the shop in the Strand. With the forceps I lift up the slug and I place him in the salt water; he dies incontinently and very neatly. My best time so far is a hundred and one in a quarter of an hour. I have found out the thing which the green fly absolutely cannot stand, and I give the green fly plenty of that thing with the syringe. I destroy earwigs. I destroy caterpillars. I have not yet reached the fine Tennysonian sensibility of the gentleman "whose eyes were tender over drowning flies." I kill some things that other things may live. They cannot all have it their own way in my garden, and I must settle which side is to prevail. All the same, I do sometimes try to look at it from the slug's point of view. What does the slug think about it? Let us hope and believe that the slug does not think about it.

With what brutality, too, does the gardener fight against the prolific impulses of nature. The dead flowers must be picked off from the sweet peas; otherwise they give up work early. If you cut down the lupine spikes as soon as the beans have formed, you will get more spikes. (I am told that this will not weaken the plant if it is well fed, but I never do it myself.) And what does it all mean, when one comes to think of it? These poor beautiful things live and struggle only for the perpetuation of their kind. When that is done, their warfare is accomplished. We make lovely gardens by thwarting and baffling this natural instinct.

Even among the plants that I tend there is civil war. My garden is surrounded by tall trees, so that at any hour of the day I can get shade. I would not have it otherwise. I would not lose one of the trees. But they are all unprincipled robbers. Their roots spread far underneath the ground. The fight goes on, and they steal the sustenance that one has given to the roses.

I knew a man who admired in his neighbour's garden the golden stars of the stone-crop. He put a little piece in an envelope and planted it in his own garden. A few years later he turned out of his garden three cartloads of stone-crop; that, I admit, was in the country. Australian bamboo is determined and rapacious. It is easy to get it into the garden. It is next to impossible to get it out. The smallest fragment of root seems to be enough, and up it comes again. The perennial sunflower is terrifically aggressive. It has a disregard of limits and wants the world. If its masses of yellow flowers were not so exhilarating, I would turn it out of my garden altogether. One would like to be able to argue with these things. I should like to say to those sunflowers: "Try to take example by the bergamot. It has the same perennial advantages as yourself, and it is quite beautiful. In addition, the scent of its leaves pressed in the fingers reminds one of Egypt. You do not find the bergamot shoving itself forward wherever it has a chance. Contemplate it and learn modesty." But argument does not avail with the perennial sunflower. The knife and the spade are the things that it understands.

I fight the weeds of course, but I have vague ideas as to what a weed is. I am quite merciless towards the bindweed, it is a murderer and a garrotter; but with the materials at my disposal I could not make anything quite so beautiful as its flowers. I found two low-growing things in a flower-bed, which seemed to be of the clover kind. One had small crimson-brown leaves with a flush of green on them; the other had a much larger green leaf with a delicate design in grey on it. The jobbing gardener said they were weeds, he would have turned them out. I saved their lives, and the one with the reddish-brown leaf rewarded me with any number of little yellow flowers. Were I a sentimentalist, I should say that this showed its gratitude. Next year some more of the same clovery thing came up in the middle of a gravel path, where it was not wanted; was that gratitude?

When one comes into my garden at the close of a fine summer day, one does really seem to come into a peaceful place apart, where the fight for life no longer exists. But the fight for life exists everywhere, and one can never get away.

Don't go, let me tell you the story of

ALFRED SIMPSON

Alfred Simpson was a nice-looking young man who had independent means and other attractions. People liked him, but when they spoke of him it was with a smile. "He is so easily influenced," said some. "He is so frightfully obstinate," said others. "He has such funny ideas," said both.

Simpson could be easily influenced by anything he saw in print. From views which he had formed in this way he could not be driven by spoken words of mature and skilled experience. He had the very unusual habit of acting upon his convictions, and the unusual is frequently funny. So possibly in what they said about Alfred Simpson people had reason.

"I have definitely made up my mind," said Alfred Simpson one day. "I will take no part whatever in the struggle. To struggle is vulgar. It happens that I have just enough to live upon; but if I had not, I should decline to earn anything. One cannot earn without beginning the struggle. Just as I set no value on property, so do I set none on my own rights. I would never resist anything."

Nobody minded. In spite of previous experience, nobody expected that Alfred Simpson would be as good as his word.

Hector Brown was quite a different type of man. His friends said that Hector was a rough diamond. His enemies said more briefly that he was a rough. Hector Brown went to a dance, danced with Mary, took her into the conservatory, and then and there kissed her—*contra pacem* and to the scandal of the Government.

Mary was very angry. She had promised to marry Alfred Simpson, and it was to him that she complained.

"Now, what you've got to do," said Alfred's friends, "is to punch Hector Brown's head."

"Why?" said Simpson.

"What will you ask next? For infringing your copyright, of course."

"That," said Simpson coldly, "would be quite contrary to the views which I have already expressed to you."

So he did not punch Hector Brown's head, and Mary told Alfred Simpson that he could go away and play by himself. Mary's decision was warmly applauded by her parents, who had heard without enthusiasm of the noble resolve on the part of their prospective son-in-law never to earn anything. Three months later Mary married Hector Brown.

Now Alfred Simpson was not a coward. He was not quite so big and heavy as Hector Brown, but he was quicker, harder, and in better training. He had been boxing while Hector had been boozing. The instructor was of opinion that Alfred could punch Hector when he liked, where he liked, and as often as he liked. Of this Alfred's friends were well aware, and it made them the more angry with him. They despaired. What could they say to a man who banged the door on the primeval instincts and declared that struggle, resistance, and retaliation were repugnant to him.

Alfred's subsequent refusal to secure a highly valuable post by the medium of a competitive examination alienated his family, as he had already alienated his friends. It is probable that his friends would have refused to have anything whatever to do with him, but for one fact—it was possible to borrow money from Alfred Simpson. They all did it, except one man, but differed in the amount and the frequency of their borrowings, according as their self-respect hindered or their necessities encouraged them. The one man who would not do it was the most confirmed borrower of them all. To the professional money-lender he was well known. "But," he said, "I cannot borrow from Alfred Simpson; it is altogether too easy—it is inartistic and gives me no satisfaction."

Without working Alfred Simpson could very well have lived on his income. But his income depended on capital, and his capital rapidly dwindled to nothing under the inroads made upon it. When his last hundred had been lent to a young gentleman who wished to test practically his solution of certain mathematical problems in the neighbourhood of Nice, Alfred Simpson went with empty pockets to those to whom he had lent money, and inquired if the repayment of the whole or part would be convenient. He returned from this inquiry with one pound six shillings, and the happy consciousness that he had not been vulgar. He had never insisted, he had never urged.

His next step was to sell the furniture of his well-appointed flat in order to pay the rent for it. After that he lived on a fairly extensive wardrobe and a few small articles of jewellery that he possessed. He retained only the gold watch and chain which had been presented to him by his mother on his twenty-first birthday.

There came a day when he had lunched lightly on his last six collars—or, to speak with pedantic accuracy, on the meal which had been provided with the money which had been acquired by the sale of those six collars. In spite of this banquet, by eight o'clock in the evening he felt hungry again, and our sentiments yield to our necessities. He therefore went out to dispose of his watch and chain. He went through Regent's Park and was stopped by a man whose appearance was against him. He looked in so many directions at once that anybody else would have mistrusted him.

"Could you tell us the time, Gov'nor?" said the man.

Alfred produced his watch. The man snatched it and the chain therewith, and ran. He did not run remarkably well. It would have been perfectly easy for Alfred Simpson to have overtaken him and to have given him into custody. But such an act would have been inconsistent with the rest of his career. So he gave up the idea of dinner and sat on the Embankment.

On the following day he remained in the parks until closing time and then sat on the Embankment again.

And the next night he dreamed that he died on the Embankment.

And after death Alfred Simpson opened his eyes and saw that he was in a large and very plainly furnished room. He sat on a hard bench, not unlike that which had been his bed on the Embankment, and many others, mostly of villainous appearance, sat there also.

"I say," said Alfred Simpson to the grey-haired reprobate next to him. "This isn't Heaven, is it?"

The reprobate chuckled. "Not exactly," he said.

"Then what is it?"

"It's the waiting-room for lost souls before they take their trial."

"But I'm not a lost soul," said Alfred Simpson indignantly. "I ought not to be here. I must have taken the wrong turning. I have never done anything very wrong in my life, and I have done heaps of good. I gave up the only girl I ever loved."

"I know," said the old man; "and in consequence she married a man she did not love out of pique. He's a brute, he ill-treats her, and she will die. You murdered her."

"This is terrible," said Alfred Simpson. "I had no idea of it. But I have done lots of other good things. I refused to go in for a competitive examination and take up a valuable post, in order that some other man might enjoy it."

"I know," said the old man again. "The other man got it; he had not your mental equipment and he was not equal to it. He bungled badly and disgraced himself. That's him over there, the man with the bullet-hole in his temples. It was his hand that held the revolver, but it was you who shot him, Alfred Simpson."

"This is most distressing," said Alfred. "If I could have foreseen this kind of thing, I should certainly have revised my ideas. I should have drawn out another scheme for my life altogether. But as it is, I must have done some good. I lent large sums of money without interest."

"I know," said the old man once more. "And by so doing you have turned various people who might have had self-respect and industry into worthless wastrels. The souls of some of them are waiting now to give evidence against you."

"It is very sad," said Alfred, "that things do not turn out as one intends. One of my last acts on earth was to allow a man to steal my watch and chain. I suppose it is useless to plead that this was a good action."

"Quite. How can you suppose it to be a good action to put such a premium on dishonesty?"

Then the door of the waiting-room opened and there stood there a most gigantic policeman.

"Alfred Simpson," he called, in a fruity and resonant voice.

"Here I am," said Alfred meekly. "Could you tell me what I am charged with?"

"You know perfectly well," said the policeman. "You are charged with starting the millennium before it was ready."

The shock awoke him. He rose and walked to his father's house. His dire necessities and abject condition broke down the alienation which had existed between him and his family, and he was welcomed as the returned prodigal. On the following morning, decently attired, with a bundle of IOU's in his pocket, he started across Regent's Park to call upon his solicitor. On his way he met a shabby man who looked in all directions at once. The shabby man saw him and ran. Alfred ran also. He caught the shabby man in an unfrequented part of the park, took from him fourpence in bronze, which was all that he possessed, and administered to him an extremely thorough hiding.

He handed the bundle of IOU's to his solicitor. Those who could pay in full were to pay in full. Those who could pay in part were to pay in part. Those who could not pay were to be left alone. Nobody was to be ruined, but Alfred Simpson was to have some of his money back.

And later, some two years later, he married the widow of Hector Brown. He is on his way to take up an important post in India, and she accompanies him. They say that she looks quite young and pretty again. She is certainly quite happy with her husband, though there are some who think him a little too selfish and dictatorial.

CHAPTER VI

NIGHT IN THE GARDEN: AND THE STORY OF "THE GHOSTLY MUSIC"

There are many things that may bring a man, normally sociable, into that state of mind when it is not desirable that he shall dine out. Too many wrong numbers on the telephone, too many visitors, too much talk—anything in fact that jangles the nerves may be the cause. In my case the cause was unimportant and uninteresting, but I was undoubtedly in that state of mind. I had to dine out, and I had not the feeling of gratitude which would have better become me. The idea of dining out filled me with rage and despair—disproportionate, ludicrous, but quite real. I recalled the words of a woman who had been through many seasons. "I want," she said to me earnestly, "to be asked to everything and to go to nothing."

And then the blessed sentence of reprieve came over the telephone. Never before had I known what a lovely word chicken-pox is. Postponed is another beautiful word; the long "o" sounds are like the coo of a dove. My more important nerves that had been revolving rapidly like large hot corkscrews began to shrink, to slow, and to cool.

Later, when it was dark, I went out into the garden. Lighted windows patterned themselves on the lawn, and half-way across it a warm wave of perfume met me from the white stars of the tobacco plants. The scents of flowers please me. Lavender and rosemary, lemon verbena and musk, rose and carnation—I have them all. But for scents in bottles or sachets, the chemist's products, I have only hatred and contempt. The bottled perfume is like mechanical music; the freshness and life have departed from it.

Even in the daytime but little sound of traffic reaches my garden, and at night there are such long stretches of precious silence that one seems to be far from London. As one grows older one values silence more—maybe a gentle providence, that in the end the great silence may not be unwelcome. The years change in so many things our sense of value. Property loses much of its attraction when one begins to think for how short a time one may hold it. This is consolatory if one be poor. I cannot own this scrap of London garden, but what matter? I may use it as if it were my own in return for—well, for so many stories a year. The transaction seems more estimable when the medium of exchange is not mentioned.

I sat and smoked, and drank the silence "like some sharp, strengthening wine". The great trees before me, motionless in the still air, were a flat dark grey against a sky a little paler. Below, where in the sunlight would be a riot of colour, were masses of velvety black out of which only the white flowers spoke. The tall white hollyhock would be a patient sentinel all night while its dark sister slept invisible. There is peace in the gardens of the country—gardens far richer and more beautiful than mine—but here the peace seemed deeper because of the near contrast. Not far away the useful deadly motor-bus would be busy for hours yet. Theatres would be full, and Fleet Street would be strenuous, and (in houses which the chicken-pox had not yet reached) people would be dining out. Perhaps, without being too artistic and diseased, one who has sometimes liked crowds may sometimes like to escape them. Dusk and sweet scents, silence and solitude—the London garden has pleasant gifts for folks who are temporarily tired of things.

Across the lighted squares or mirrored windows on the lawn, slow yet alert, crept a cat with a heart full of sinful purposes. It flickered over the wall, poised clear against the sky for one moment, on its way to blood and passion in some valerian-scented hell. The nocturnal cat is supposed to be comic, but (in spite of many opportunities) I have never managed to see the joke. There is something terrific in those lower animals—there are several of them—that in certain moments produces the sound of the human voice. Strange too is that electric repugnance that a cat may set up. Unseen and unheard, her presence is yet felt and loathed. She is a creature of the night, mysterious and satanic. Watch her as she starts for the black sabbath—a voluptuous sprawl with claws extended, steps of tense and measured stealth, and then a mad scurry. Presently, you shall hear her cry like a woman, even as the wounded hare sobs out her sisterhood. To-night it was as though for a few moments a taint of monstrousness had passed through the peace of the garden.

Through an open window not far away came the sound of music—somebody was playing the piano. Music heard from another house is supposed to be a torture, and so (like the cat) has its place among the accepted jokes. But, because to-night I was to have the luck—who invented chicken-pox?—it was not distressing and funny. It was fine music played by an artist on a good instrument. It had the quality of the night, wistful and desiderious. Long ago and in a far country there was a king who suffered from a restless melancholy, or a bad temper, or something of that kind, and somebody made music for him. "So Saul was refreshed, and was well, and the evil spirit departed from him." Surely, that nocturne was meant to be heard as I heard it—in a garden at night. Alas, these concerts, with their awful too-muchness, and professional smirks, and roars of ugly applause! I do not like to have music thus administered. But for the music that visited my garden that night I had the most grateful welcome.

When the chance things are charming they far surpass the calculated, and love itself may be no more than a delightful accident. It was just by chance that somebody in a lighted room, without a thought of audience, went to the piano and remembered that music. Chance makes things grow on old stone walls; and in the rich man's rock-garden, wealth, skill, and calculation try to imitate the charm. The music ceased, and my gratitude must remain unspoken— unless, by a chance that were wellnigh miraculous, this page may carry it. But artists—be they makers of music or pictures, poems or stories—must not think too much of gratitude; for they will not always get it, and they will not always deserve it. That king of old once flung a javelin at the musician who played before him. Some lazy souls can never do their uttermost unless they are thrashed up to it. A moderate amount of javelin—avoiding vital parts—is not always bad for the artist.

My garden, they tell me, was once the garden of an old priory. Under one corner of the lawn is the well that provided the religious with water. It has been covered in with stone, and just over the stone the grass refuses to grow. It is like a tonsure. But though I have been in my garden I think at every hour of the night and of the early morning, I have met no shadowy figures counting their beads or reading their little illuminated books. These good people sleep long and quietly.

Let me tell you the story of

THE GHOSTLY MUSIC

There was once a master of music, who, from the charity of his heart and from his love of excellence, took as his pupil without reward a young boy that was greatly gifted. And in time it came to pass that the pupil reached his zenith and the powers of the master had begun to decline, so that it was said by some that the pupil now surpassed the master. And the hints of this that came to the master's ears were to him bitter as wormwood.

Now it happened one day that, as the pupil walked in a wood, music came to him; and he hastened back to his house in order that he might sit down at the piano and play it. For although, being a musician, he knew quite well how the music would sound, he yet wished to hear it. And as he was on his way, though it was a calm day, the great limb of a treacherous elm fell upon him and crushed him so that he died. And in his music-room his piano waited in vain.

Upon his death all bitterness passed away from the heart of his master. Rivalry died with the rival. There came back to him old recollections of the boy and of the esteem and affection in which he had then held him. There was now no one who spoke of the dead musician with more generous praise than his master. In his own music-room the master placed the piano on which his pupil had been used to play. It had been specially bequeathed to him. It was the dead man's gift.

But now the old man became himself conscious that he was not as he had been. The fountains were dried up. Melody had ceased to come. He was arid and unproductive. His fear that his power was leaving him tended the more to diminish it. There were many long days and nights when he could do nothing; and at such seasons he would not enter his music-room upstairs, but sat in the room below it, trying sometimes to divert his mind by reading, and at other times cursing the wretchedness into which the course of nature had brought him.

After a long while it happened that one night when he sat late alone, his wretchedness seemed to him more than he could bear. In a few weeks he was to play before the King and there would be many great musicians in the audience. On such occasions it had always been his custom to produce some new work. Now he had nothing to give them. He would have to fall back on the compositions of his younger days. He could picture in his mind the meaning looks which the musicians would interchange. He could hear their polite applause, and it was like a torture. The King, himself no mean musician, might ask some question. He could not go into that company and thus fail. It was not possible. It could not be asked of him thus to debase himself. And there seemed to him but one alternative—a little more than usual of that laudanum in which he had lately sought inspiration.

But as he raised the glass to his lips he heard something so unexpected that the glass crashed to the floor. In the music-room overhead someone was playing the piano. Who could it be? No servant of his had that skill, and besides, hours before his servants had gone to sleep. It was divine music, entrancing, uplifting.

For a moment he hesitated, and then the desire to know overcame his fears. He went up the stairs, and in the passage outside the music-room he noted that a light showed under the door. Someone had switched the light on then. Was it the carelessness of a servant? "Quite possibly," he said to himself. "Quite possibly."

He opened the door and entered, and his eyes flew to the piano. No one was seated there, but the notes moved and the touch was human. He shrank back from the piano and stood in the farthest corner of the room, listening intently. When at last the music ceased, he had a great desire to say something, and yet could choose no words. And, as he hesitated, there was a sudden click and the lights were switched off. He fled from the darkness down the stairs to the brightly lit room below. For a while he was too overcome to be able to do anything; and then, for he had a musician's memory, he took paper and wrote down the music that he had heard.

A few days later it chanced that a great lady asked him what new music he would play before the King.

"I have decided," said the master, "to play a composition of mine that—if one must give these things names—I shall call 'The Sylvan Sonata'."

"Sylvan? How delightful. It represents scenes in the wood then."

The master shook his head. "Music represents nothing," he said. "Music is music. It is not an imitation of a sylvan scene, or church bells heard in the distance, or any other rubbish. I call this music 'The Sylvan Sonata' merely because it has in it different phases of woodland feeling. You understand me? It is the kind of music that might occur to the mind of a musician when he was walking through a wood."

"But how that reminds one," said the great lady. "It was in the wood that your favourite pupil died."

"I prefer," said the master sternly, "not to speak of that."

He preferred also not to think of it. The piano which had been bequeathed to him was kept closed and locked now, and it was on another instrument in another room that he prepared himself for the great occasion. He was a fine executant, as not every composer is. He tried to cheat himself. He said again and again to himself that what he had seen and heard in the music-room that night was illusion. The notes had not really moved. His brain had been over-wrought with worry and anxiety. The music was really his own. But the attempt to cheat himself was idle, for he knew too much of the characteristics of a promising young composer who was now dead. No one else but him could have written that.

The evening came and the occasion found him equal to it. His playing of "The Sylvan Sonata" was as near perfection as a man may attain. When he had finished there were a few seconds of silence before the audience could get back to the world again and begin their applause. And when that had died away, many came up to congratulate him, and a critic of music spoke.

"I am ashamed of myself," said the critic. "I confess that I had thought, in company with many others, that you declined in power, *maestro*. You have given us to-night something more superb than we have ever heard from you before. You are at your very highest at this minute."

The master did not seem to hear, did not seem to see the hands which were stretched out to him. He sat looking intently before him, as at some presence not visible to the others. And when he was summoned to speak to the King, he rose stiffly and moved mechanically, looking now and again over his shoulder, as at someone who followed him.

And when the King had finished his compliments, he drew a deep breath, as of one who makes an effort. He swung round and pointed with a wave of his hand.

"Alas, sir," he said, "I am not he who made 'The Sylvan Sonata'. But the composer is here. See him. He stands behind me. The face was somewhat crushed by the fall of the tree, but it is made well again. It is as it always was. It is his music, not mine, that I have played to you."

He stepped backward from the royal presence. The shiver of sensation went through the great assembly. This was clearly aberration. Someone should see to the old man. The trial had been too great for him, and his reason had been overcome. A doctor should be summoned.

But before anything could be done, the old man had slipped out of the assembly and left the palace and gone back to his own house. Once more he poured the laudanum, and this time his hand did not fail him. When he had drunk, he went up to the music-room again and unlocked the piano that had once been his pupil's. He opened it and began to play.

It was there they found him in the morning.

It was late at night and I had gone out to see the September moon. It was one of those nights which people like to say are as light as day. It was not in the least as light as day. It was light grey and silver. It was even black in places. I heard a faint crackle and could smell the acrid smoke which mounted thin and straight in the still air from the fire which had been made in the morning. There burned things which had done their work and had been beautiful, but were now over.

The fire had been lit that morning and the lawn had been swept that morning; but there was a rustle of fallen leaves about my feet. The air was shrewd and chill. Next morning I should still see flowers in my garden, but none the less the sentence had been pronounced. Summer was dead.

I suppose it is a question of temperament. Youth can enjoy the moment. Age must look forward. There is plenty of work to do in this garden in the autumn, and not a little in the winter. And all the time one is looking forward to the spring—to the coming of the new leaves and the fresh green.

But then, throughout the summer, one is haunted with fear and hatred of the coming winter. Even as one plants or sows, one seems to see the September weed fire.

It is better not to be wearisome, sentimental, and self-pitying on the subject, for one might get into that state of mind when, throughout the winter, one would no longer dare to look forward to the summer, because one would know the summer would be haunted with the hatred of the next winter. From which refinement and desolation may I be delivered.

ZERO

CHAPTER I

James Smith was a trainer and exhibitor of performing dogs. His age was forty-five, but on the stage he looked less, moving always with an alertness suggestive of youth. His face was dominant, but not cruel. He never petted a dog. On the other hand, he never thrashed a dog, unless he considered that the dog had deserved it. He had small eyes and a strong jaw. He was somewhat undersized, and his body was lean and hard. This afternoon, clad in a well-cut flannel suit, and wearing a straw hat, he sat on the steps of a bathing-machine on the beach at Helmstone. He was waiting for the man inside the machine to come out. Meanwhile he made himself a cigarette, rolling it on his leg with one hand, and securing the paper by a small miracle instead of by gum.

As he lit the cigarette the door of the bathing-machine opened, and a tall young man of athletic build came out. He was no better dressed than James Smith. At the same time, it was just as obvious that he was a gentleman as that Smith was not.

"Hallo!" said the young man. "You're all right again, I see. What was it—touch of cramp?"

"No, sir," said Smith. "I'm not a strong swimmer, and I've done no sea bathing before. I never meant to get out of my depth, but the current took me. What I want now is to do something to show my gratitude."

"Gratitude be blowed!" said the young man cheerfully. "It was no trouble to me, and I happened to be there."

"Well, sir," said Smith, "will you let me give you a dog? I've got some very good dogs. I should take it as a favour if you would."

He took from a Russia leather case a clean professional card, and presented it to the young man.

"That, of course, is not my real name. That's just the French name they've put on the programmes. I'm James Smith, and I have a two weeks' engagement at the Hippodrome here. I've got my dogs in a stable not far from there."

The young man glanced at his watch.

"Well," he said, "I've got nothing to do this morning, I'll go and have a look at the dogs, at any rate. They're a pretty clever lot, I suppose."

"They can do what they've been taught," said Smith; "all except one of them, and he can do what no man can teach him."

There was a great noise when they entered the stables. Twenty dogs, most of them black poodles, all tried to talk at once. Smith said something decisively, but quietly, and the dogs became silent again. Smith made a sign to one of the poodles and held out his walking-stick. It looked quite impossible, but the dog went over it.

"My word, but that's a wonderful jump!" said the young man.

"It is," said Smith. "You won't find another dog of that breed in this country that can do the same. He's yours, if you like to take him."

"No; hang it all! I'm not going to do that. I'm not going to take a dog which you can use professionally. What about the beggar that you said you could not teach?"

Smith pointed to a huge brindled bulldog, who lay in one corner of the stable absolutely motionless, watching them intently.

"That's the one," lie said. "He's never been on the stage at all. He couldn't even be taught to fetch and carry."

"And you just keep him because you're fond of him?"

"Fond of him? No, I'm not fond of dogs. They're my livelihood, and I don't do so badly out of it. But I'm not fond of 'em—know too much about 'em."

"Then what do you keep him for?"

"You may call it a sense of justice, or you may call it curiosity. He's a rum 'un, that dog is, and no mistake."

"In what way rum?"

"I'll tell you. He's a dog that sees dangers ahead. He knows when things are going to happen. I had him as a puppy, and when I found I could teach him nothing, I made up my mind to get quit of him. I was going off by train that day to a village fifteen miles away, and I knew a man there who I thought might take a fancy to Zero."

"Zero, you call him?"

"Yes; that was a bit of my fun. As a performing dog he was just absolutely last—number naught, see? Well, as I was saying, there was I on the platform with the dog at my heel and the ticket in my hand. Just as I was going to get into the train, he made a jump for that ticket, caught it in his mouth and bolted with it, nipping in among a lot of milk-cans. I called him, and he wouldn't come out. Then I went in after him, and he bolted again. By the time I did get him I had missed my train, and I didn't give him half a jolly good hiding for it, I don't think! If I'd gone by that train I shouldn't have been talking to you now. Collision three miles from the station. Well, you don't apologise to a dog. All I could do was to keep him. But that wasn't the only instance. The beggar knows things."

"Apparently he didn't know that you were going to drown yourself this morning."

"If he knew anything about it, he knew that I wasn't."

"Good-tempered dog?"

"Oh, all bulldogs are safe! You want to look after him with collies. He doesn't like 'em. If he gets hold of one, it's bad for the collie. Otherwise a baby could handle him."

Zero had crossed over to them, and the young man stooped down and patted him. The dog expressed delight.

"I can send him round to your hotel," said Smith; "or, for that matter, he'd follow you. He's taken a fancy to you, he has."

"Look here," said the young man, "let me buy him. I'm not a millionaire, but I can afford to buy a dog. I'd like to have this one, and there's no reason on earth why you should give him to me."

"You'd like to have him, and I can afford to give him to you, and I want to give him to you. You must let a man indulge his sense of gratitude. It's only fair."

"Very well, if you say so. Many thanks. I'll step over to the Hippodrome and see your show to-night."

"Do. You'll be surprised."

The two men talked for a few moments longer, and then Zero's new owner said that he must be getting back to lunch.

"You really think the dog will follow me?" he said. "I don't want to take a lead?"

"I know he'll follow you. I tell you I know dogs. They take fancies sometimes. You can take that dog out, and if I call him back myself he wouldn't come."

"I bet you a sovereign he would."

"I'll take that," said Smith. "You go on with him, and I'll wait here."

The young man walked a few yards away with the dog at his heels, and then Smith called the dog back, loudly and insistently. The dog did not give the slightest sign that he had heard anything at all. When his master stood still, he remained standing patiently at his heel, and never once looked back.

The young man laughed as he took out his sovereign-case.

"Queer chap, Zero. Well, you've won, Mr Smith. Catch!"

Mr Smith caught the sovereign adroitly, and went back into the stable.

"Yes," he said to the cleverest of the black poodles, "I don't know that I wouldn't sooner he'd taken you."

It was seldom that Smith addressed any of his dogs, except to give an order. The poodle did not know what to make of it. He whined faintly.

Richard Staines went back to his hotel, with Zero at his heels. He had his own sitting-room opening into his bedroom at the hotel, and he intended to keep the dog there at night. This was against the laws of the hotel; therefore Staines had to pause a few moments in the hall to get the laws altered. One of the arguments he used was that he would only be there two days longer, and it would not matter for so short a time. The other argument was bribery and corruption. After which he and Zero went up in the lift together.

CHAPTER II

Staines was a partner in succession to his father in an old-established firm of stockbrokers with a good connection. He had a small flat in St James's Place, and thither he brought Zero. Zero accepted metropolitan life philosophically. There was a dingy cat in the basement of St James's Place, and he was quite willing to make friends with her. He looked mildly puzzled at her definite assurance that she would kill him if he came a step nearer. It never occurred to him to attempt to injure her. But for one slight lapse—he had killed a collie, and cost Staines compensation—his behaviour was admirable. He was fortunate in having a master who was fond of outdoor life, and not at all fond of London. Every week-end, and occasionally on a fine afternoon, if business was slack, he got away into the country. He never quite seemed to understand the terror which his appearance inspired in some young or foolish people. When children rushed from him shrieking, he would look up at his master as much as to say, "Can you understand this?" And he was careful not to increase their terror by running after them.

One day in the Park a muddy-faced little girl of six, who feared nothing at all, came up and patted him, examined his teeth with curious interest, and finally sat on him. These attentions Zero received with great joy. Weeks passed, and he had not given the slightest sign of the curious instinct with which his former master had credited him.

Staines liked him, principally because he so obviously liked Staines. Staines thought him a faithful and affectionate beast, with nothing to distinguish him from the normal. When he recalled Smith's story of the snatched railway ticket, he explained it all as a chance. These flukes did happen sometimes.

And then one afternoon he went to call upon the Murrays—a practice that was becoming rather common with him—and as Jane was particularly fond of Zero, Zero accompanied him. When they reached the square, Zero sat down on the pavement. Staines called him, and the dog wagged his tail, but did not move. Staines went on without him, but presently had to stop, for Zero had now changed his tactics, and was running round and round Staines' legs. The incident of the railway ticket flashed across his mind. He was a business man, and not superstitious; however, it did not matter to him in the least which two sides of the square he took, and he determined to turn back and take the other two sides, and see what would happen. As soon as he turned back, Zero followed at heel in his usual quiet and unobtrusive manner.

A loud crash caused him to look round. A heavy stone coping had fallen from a roof, and if the dog had not brought him back it would have fallen upon him. Here was a nice little story with a mildly sensational interest for Staines to tell over the teacups.

Mr Murray was matter-of-fact.

"Your story is true, of course," he said. "Your dog did make you take the other two sides of the square, and the fact that you turned back probably saved your life. But, all the same, the dog didn't know. By what means could the brain of a dog recognise the imminent dissolution of part of the roof of a house?"

"Zero did know," said Jane. She was Mr Murray's only daughter, and without being wildly beautiful, was an extremely pleasing and friendly young woman to look at. At present she was feeding Zero with thin bread-and-butter. Zero had been told, even by Jane herself, that this form of diet was bad for his figure, but he accepted it with resignation—rather an enthusiastic kind of resignation.

"What makes you say that Zero knew?" her father asked, with indulgent superiority.

"Because I know he knew," said Jane firmly and finally.

"And then," said Mr Murray, "women tell us they ought to have the vote."

"Miss Murray," said Richard firmly, "that dog is not to be fed any more, please."

"Last piece," said Jane. "And he's promised to do Swedish exercises."

Richard was inclined to agree with Mr Murray. The coincidence was again remarkable; it might even be called very extraordinary. And, given a choice of two things, Richard preferred to believe the easier. Why, fond though he was of Zero, he had to admit that the dog was not even clever.

He had tried to teach Zero to find a hidden biscuit, but though he had hidden the biscuit in all manner of places he had never yet selected a place that Zero had been able to discover. He was just a dear old fool of a bulldog, and it was absurd to suppose that he was a miracle.

But Jane Murray remained firm in her belief, and even condescended to be serious about it.

"Look here," she said, "if you put your horse at a jump, and you're feeling a bit shy of it yourself, do you mean to say the horse doesn't know?"

"Of course he knows. But he only knows it by the way you ride him."

"Well, I've had it happen to me. All I can say is that I wasn't conscious of riding any differently. It was my first season in Ireland, and I wasn't used to the walls. I said to myself, 'It's got to be.' I did really mean to get over. But the horse knew the funk in my head and refused. However, I'll give you another point. How do you explain the homing instinct of animals?"

"I've never thought about it. I suppose when a pigeon gets up high it can see no end of a distance."

"That won't do. Dogs and cats have the same instinct—especially cats. For that matter, crabs have been taken from the sea and returned to it again at a point eighty miles away, and have found their way back. It's not done by sight, scent, or hearing. It must be done by some special sense which they have got and we have not."

"It sounds plausible."

"It's the only possible explanation. And when once we've admitted that animals have a special sense which we have not, I don't quite see how we are to say what the limitations of that sense are. It is not really a bit more wonderful that Zero should have the sense of impending danger than that a crab, eighty miles from home, should be able to find its way back."

"Well, you may be right. I wish now that I'd asked that chap Smith a bit more about the dog."

A few days later one of the partners in Richard's business announced his intention of getting married. He was a junior partner, two years younger than Richard.

"Well, Bill," said Richard, after he had offered his congratulations, "what shall I give you for a wedding-present?"

"Give us that dog of yours."

"Never. Try again."

"Oh, I was only rotting. But, seriously, I'd as soon have a dog as anything. Not a bulldog—they're too ugly."

"It's a good, honest kind of ugliness. What breed then?"

"Gwen's keen on black poodles."

That settled it. Richard hunted up Smith's card. He had always meant to do some business with the man if he got an opportunity, and here was the opportunity. On the following day he journeyed to Wandsworth and found Smith. Smith looked less spruce and prosperous than before. He did not actually declare that the performing dog had had his day, but he admitted that business was not what it had been.

"Too many of us in it. And, I tell you, I'm afraid to bring out a new idea—it's pinched before you've had a week's use of it. Public's a bit off it, too. I'm doing practically nothing with the 'alls. I train for others, and I'm trying to build up a business as a dealer. Only first-class dogs, mind."

"That's what I want. I came here to buy a dog."

"Let's see. Bulldogs were your fancy. Well, I've got one of the Stone breed that's won the only time it was shown and will win again."

"This is not for myself. It's a present. Black poodle."

"I see. Well, you've come to the right market. How far were you prepared to go?"

"Show me a really valuable dog and I will pay the real value. I'm not buying for the show-bench; but I want the best breed, good health, good temper, cleverness and training—two years old for choice."

"Ask enough," said Smith, smiling. "Well, if you don't mind stepping into the yard I can fit you. I'm asking twenty guineas, and he's worth every penny of it—he'd bring that money back, to anybody who cared to take it, before a year was out."

The dog was shown—an aristocrat with qualities of temper and intelligence not always to be found in the aristocrat. Richard Staines thought he would be paying quite enough, but decided to pay it. He returned to the house to write his cheque.

"There you are, Mr Smith. By the way, do you remember Zero, the dog you gave me? He's sitting in my taxi outside."

"I remember him. He'd never win prizes for anybody—not like that poodle you've just bought. You couldn't teach him anything either. But he could see ahead, that dog could."

Smith heard how Richard Staines had been saved from the falling roof, and evinced no surprise at it at all. "Yes," he said, "that dog always knew. Did I tell you about the milk?"

"No. What was that?"

"Me and Cowbit next door got our milk from the same man. I went out one morning to take the can in, when Zero came bullocking past me and knocked the can over. He never tried to drink the milk that was spilled, but just stood there, wagging his old tail. Mind you, sir, that was after he had saved me from the train smash. 'Well,' I said to him, 'I suppose you know'; and I went in to Cowbits' to tell them not to touch that milk. Cowbit laughed at the story, and took milk in his tea. But his missus wouldn't have any, and wouldn't let the baby have none either. Cowbit was ill for days and pretty near died. Mineral poison it was, from one of the milk-pans going wrong."

"How do you suppose the dog knew?"

"Me suppose? Why, I never asked myself the question. He did know—that was all about it. Still, if I had to explain it, I should say it was some kind of an instinct."

And Richard mercifully forebore to ask Mr Smith how he would explain that particular kind of instinct.

CHAPTER III

Richard was best-man at his partner's wedding. He afterwards attended a crowded reception. It was too crowded; and there were far too many people there who wanted to talk to Jane Murray. She was popular, and there was a group round her all the time. Not for five minutes could Richard get her to himself. It was this selfishness on the part of others which depressed him, not the reception champagne, which was no worse than is usual on such occasions.

The crowds bored him and when he got back to his flat the solitude bored him. Not even Zero was there. Richard's valet had taken the dog out for exercise; this had been done in obedience to Richard's own orders, but it now seemed to him in the light of a grievance. The grievance became more acute when his servant returned without the dog.

"Very sorry, sir; I wouldn't have had it happen for anything. I was walking in Regent's Park, with the dog at my heels, and all of a sudden he made a bolt for it. I whistled and called, but he went straight on. And when I started running after him, he made a dash into a big shrubbery. That was how he foxed me, sir. While I was hunting him on one side, he must have bolted out on the other. Never known the dog act like that before. It was just as if something had come over him. Speaking in a general way—"

"Well, what did you do?" asked Richard sharply.

"I spoke to the park-keepers, and to a couple of policemen outside, and then I went on to Scotland Yard. The address is on the collar, sir. I should think there's no doubt you'll—"

"That'll do!" snapped Richard. "I thought you could be trusted to take a dog out, at any rate. Well, my mistake."

With a further expression of contrition, the man withdrew, and almost instantly the telephone-bell on Richard's desk rang sharply.

He went slowly to the telephone, and managed to put the concentration of weariness and disgust into the word "Hallo!"

The voice that answered him was the voice of Mr Murray.

"That you, Staines? ... Right—yes, quite well, thanks.... I wanted to say when Jane got back this evening she found Zero waiting for her outside our front door.... He's here now, and seems quite cheerful about it.... Thought you might like to know."

Richard rapidly changed his tone of dejection for that of social enthusiasm. He thanked profusely. He would send for the dog at once.

"Well, look here," said Mr Murray, "Jane and I have got a night off—dining alone. If by any chance you're free, I wish you'd join us. Then you can take the intelligent hound back with you."

Richard said that he was free, which was a lie; and that he would be delighted to come, which was perfectly true.

He subsequently rang up a man at his club, cancelled an engagement on the score of ill-health, and went to dress. Such was his elation that he even condescended to tell his servant that the dog had been found and was all right.

Zero had done wrong. He must have known that he had done wrong; but he welcomed his master with gambols in the manner of an ecstatic bullock, and showed no sign of penitence at all. It was the habit of Richard to punish a dog that had done wrong, but he did not punish Zero. He called him a silly old idiot, and asked him what he thought he had been doing, but Zero recognised that this was badinage and exercised his tail furiously.

At dinner, Mr Murray said that Zero was an interesting problem. The dog was apparently a fine judge at sight of the stability of structures, but could not find his way home.

"That's not proved," said Richard, laughing. "He knew his way home all right, but he was trying to better himself. He's not fed at tea-time in St James's Place."

"He's had nothing here," said Jane.

"Really, Jane," said her father.

"Practically nothing. A few biscuits and the least little bit of wedding-cake for luck."

"Pity I didn't take him to the reception; then he could have had a vanilla ice as well."

"Wrong," said Jane. "They hadn't got vanilla—only the esoteric sorts. I know, because I tried. Never you mind, Zero. When the election comes on, you shall wear papa's colours round your strengthy neck and kill all the collies of the opposition."

"By the way," said Richard, "how's old Benham?"

"Poor old chap, he's still dying," said Mr Murray. "It makes me feel a bit like a vulture, waiting for his death like this. Still, I suppose it can't be helped."

Benham was the sitting member for Sidlington, and Mr Murray had been predestined to succeed him. Murray had fought two forlorn hopes for his party, and had pulled down majorities. He had fairly earned Sidlington—an absolutely safe seat. He had moderate means and no occupation. He had taken up with politics ten years before—shortly after the death of his wife—and had found politics a game that precisely suited him.

The discussion for the remainder of dinner was mostly political, and Jane—as was generally the case when she chose to be serious—showed herself to be a remarkably well-informed and intelligent young woman.

"I've no chance; she's too good for me," said Richard to himself—by no means for the first time—as he looked at her and listened to her with admiration.

Jane had just left the two men to their cigars when a servant entered with a card for Mr Murray.

"Where have you put him?" he asked the man.

"The gentleman is in the library, sir."

"Good! Say I'll be with him directly. Awfully sorry, Staines; this is a chap from Sidlington, and rather an important old cock down there."

"Go to him, of course. That's all right."

"I'm afraid I must. But here's the port and here's the cigars. When you get tired of solitude, you'll find Jane in the drawing-room. Smoking's allowed there, you know."

Staines got tired of solitude very soon. In the drawing-room, the conversation between Jane and himself took a new note of earnestness and intimacy. Zero slept placidly through it all.

An hour later Mr Murray came back to the drawing-room with the news of Benham's death. He in return received, with goodwill and no surprise, the news that a marriage bad been arranged, and would shortly take place, between his daughter and Richard Staines.

CHAPTER IV

During the engagement, which was brief, Zero found that two people—of whom his master was one—had very little time to talk to him; but he was not absolutely forgotten.

"What are we to do with Zero while we're away?" asked Richard.

"Could we take him with us?" asked Miss Murray.

"I don't think so," said Richard. "There would be bother at these foreign hotels; and there's the quarantine to think about."

"Suppose I said that if Zero didn't go, I wouldn't go either?"

"Quite simple. In that case, I should go alone."

And then they both laughed, being somewhat easily pleased at that time. Zero was offered to Mr Murray temporarily as an election mascot, but Mr Murray was not taking any risks—one of his principal supporters had a favourite collie. Finally, it was decided that Zero should pay a visit to his former master, Smith, until his master returned. He made one brief appearance at the wedding reception, where his supreme but honest ugliness conquered the heart of every nice woman present. He refused champagne, foie-gras sandwiches, and vanilla ices offered to him by the enthusiastic and indiscreet. However, he managed to find Jane, and Jane found bread-and-butter until word was brought that a person of the name of Smith had called for the dog.

"Bit fat, you are," said Smith, as he ripped the white rosette off the dog's collar. "Been doing yourself too well. Ah, now you're going to live healthy!"

Smith was as good as his word. Zero was sufficiently and properly fed, and given plenty of exercise. He mixed with some very aristocratic canine society, where the sweetness of his temper was much commended and imposed upon. After two months his master called for him, and Zero once more behaved like an ecstatic bullock.

"Yes," said Smith, "he's in good condition, as you say. Otherwise, he's not much changed. He's as big a fool as ever he was. If a toy Pom growls at him, he runs away; and if a collie tries to get past him alive—well, it can't. He'd tear the throat out of any man as struck you, and if the cat next door spits at him he goes and hides in the rhubarb."

"Seen any more of that wonderful instinct of his?"

"No, sir, I have not. But I should have done if there had been any occasion for it. It's a fact that I never feel so safe as I do when I've got that dog here. Don't you believe in it yourself, sir?"

"Sometimes I do—Mrs Staines does absolutely. If there's nothing in it, then there has been the most extraordinary lot of coincidences I ever came across."

Richard Staines and his wife had agreed that they would live principally in the country, and one day during their engagement Jane took Richard down to Selsdon Bois to show him the house of her dreams, known to the Post Office as Midway. Then, when he came to select, he would know the kind of thing to look for. Jane had known Midway in her childhood, and had loved its wide and gentle staircases, its fine Jacobean panelling, its stone roof, and its old garden with the paved walks between yew hedges.

"Well," said Richard, "if you are so keen on the place, why shouldn't we wait for a chance to get it, instead of looking for something more or less like it?"

"Because you can't," said Jane. "We're general public, and general public is never allowed to buy a place like Midway. People live in it till they die, and then leave it to the person they love best, and that person lives in it till he dies. And so on again. It never comes into the market. Things that are really valuable hardly ever do."

The conversation took place in the train which was conveying them to Selsdon Bois.

"Ah, well," said Richard, "what is there? It needn't be very big to be too big for us."

"Not a big house at all. I never counted, but I should think about twenty rooms." She made guesses as to acreage of garden, orchard, and grass-land. She admitted that they were merely guesses.

"The only thing that I really remember is that it was thirty-six acres in all. Could we do it?"

"Yes," said Richard; "we ought to be able to do that."

"Still, it doesn't matter," said Jane despondently, "because, of course, places like that are never to be got."

Then they stepped out on to the platform of Selsdon Bois Station, where a man was busily pasting up a bill. It announced the sale by auction, unless previously disposed of, of Midway.

"Miracle!" said Jane, subsiding gracefully on to a milk-can. "It's ours!"

And a fortnight later it was really theirs. The house was as delightful as Jane had said, but it was an old house, and during the last ten years had not been well kept up. There was a good deal to be done to make it quite comfortable and satisfactory. The work was to have been finished by the time Richard and his wife returned from the honeymoon.

"It's been simply funny the way we've been kept back," said the builder cheerfully. "But you might be able to get in, say, in another week or so."

They remained for a month in town, and this gave Jane time to discover that it was not possible to teach Zero to do trust-and-paid-for, and to look up a really admirable train by which Richard might travel from Selsdon Bois to the city every weekday morning.

"Yes," said Richard, a little doubtfully, "it's quite a good train, but—"

"But what?"

"Oh, nothing. I shall probably take it whenever I go up, though it's a bit earlier than is absolutely necessary. You see, I don't regard my presence at the office as so essential as I once did. My partners are most able and trustworthy men, and they like the work. Of course, I shall keep an eye on things."

"Then how many days a week will you go up?"

"Well, just at first I shall go up—er—from time to time."

"Come here, Zero," said Jane. "See that man? He's idle. Kill him!"

"Idle? Why, I shall have any amount of things to do down at Midway! Gardeners and grooms want a deal of looking after at first, until they pick up the way you want things done. Then there's that car your father gave us. I've got to learn how to drive it; I've got to know all about its blessed works right up to the very last word. The man who don't is open to be robbed and fooled by his chauffeur. That won't be done in a week. Then I've had an idea that we might lay out a golf-course—quite a small affair, just for practice."

"Richard, you're a genius! (You needn't bite him after all, Zero.) That will be the very thing for guests on Sunday afternoons—not to mention us ourselves."

"I was thinking principally of us ourselves."

"Where is that big-scale plan of the land? We'll pin it down flat on the table, and start arranging it now. We shall probably have to alter it all afterwards, but that don't matter."

CHAPTER V

Six years had passed; and Zero had got a new master, a somewhat dictatorial gentleman, but with genuine goodness of heart, aged five, bearing the same name as his father, Richard Staines, but never by any chance addressed by it. His father called him Dick. His mother called him by various fond and foolish appellations. He was known to the servants of the household as the Emperor. He had two sisters, whom he always spoke of collectively as "the children." He always spoke of Zero as "my dog."

Zero was rather an old dog now, but hale and hearty. In his own circle he was highly valued, but his formidable appearance still struck terror among strangers, willing though he was to make friends with them. The tradespeople, who had at first approached very delicately, had now grown used to him; but the tramp or hawker who entered the garden at Midway, and found Zero looking at him pensively, as a rule retired quickly to see if the road was still there. No further instance had occurred of Zero's mysterious powers, and in consequence they tended to become legendary. Richard Staines had now definitely adopted the theory of coincidence.

"Zero's a good old friend of mine, and I love him," he said; "but we must give up pretending he's a miracle." Jane's faith, however, remained unshaken.

And then, one summer evening, Dick came into the drawing-room with determination in his face.

"Mother," he said, "I want a stick or whip, please."

"Well, now," said Jane, "what for?"

"To beat my dog with. He's got to be punished."

"That's a pity, Dickywick. What's he been doing?"

"He won't let me go out into the road. Every time he caught hold of my coat and pulled me back. He's most frightfully strong, and he pulled me over once. He wants a lamming."

"I wonder if he would let me go out," said Jane. "Let's go and see, shall we?"

"Right-oh," said Dick, perfectly satisfied.

In the garden they found Zero cheerful and quite unrepentant. As a rule, he rushed to the gate in the hopes of being taken out for a run. But this evening, as Jane neared the gate, he became disquieted. He caught hold of her dress and tried to drag her back. He ran round and round her, whimpering. He flung himself in front of her feet.

"Now, you see," said Dick triumphantly.

"Yes, I see."

"Well, I shall go and fetch a stick."

"Oh, no. Zero does not want us to go out because he believes there's some danger on the road."

"O-o-oh! Do you really mean it?"

"Honest Injun."

"Then he's not a bad dog at all, and I told him he was. Come here, Zero." He patted the dog's head. "You're a good dog really. My mistake. Sorry. What are you laughing at, mother? That's what Tom always says. Now let's go and see the danger on the road."

"Well, it wouldn't be quite fair to Zero, after all the trouble he's taken. Besides, I want to see the rabbits at their games. They ought to be out just now."

"All right," said Dick. "You follow me, and I'll show you them. But you mustn't make the least sound. You must be very Red-Indian."

Dick's mother followed him obediently, and was very Red-Indian. The rabbits lived in a high bank just beyond the far end of the garden, and what the gardener had said about them before the wire-netting came could not be printed. Jane watched the rabbits, and conversed about them in the hoarse whisper enjoined by her son, but she was thinking principally about Zero.

Then Dick went to bed, and his father came back from the city. He went up at least one day a week, and came back full of aggressive virtue and likely to refer to himself as a man who earned his own living, thank Heaven.

At dinner Richard said: "By the way, I'd been meaning to speak of it—what's the matter with Zero?"

"Why?"

"He won't leave the gate. He was there when I drove in. I called him in, but he went back almost directly. I saw him through the window as I was dressing, and he was still there—lying quite still, with his eyes glued on the road."

And then Jane recounted the experience of Dick and herself.

"You may laugh, Richard, but something is going to happen, and Zero knows what it will be."

"Well," said Richard, "if anybody is proposing to burglarise us to-night, I don't envy him the preliminaries with Zero. But, of course, it may be nothing. All the same I've always said there ought to be a lodge at that gate."

But to this Jane was most firmly opposed. A new semi-artistic red-brick lodge would be out of keeping with Midway altogether. "And what are you going to do about Zero?"

"Oh, anything you like. What do you propose?"

"I don't know what to say. Whatever is going to happen, apparently Zero thinks he can tackle it by himself. Still, you might have your revolver somewhere handy to-night."

"I will," said Richard.

Zero remained at his post until the dawn, and then came a black speck on the white road. Zero stood up and growled. The skin on his back moved.

Down the road came the lean, black retriever, snapping aimlessly, foam dropping from his jaws. Zero sprang at him and was thrown down and bitten. At his second spring he got hold and kept it. The two dogs rolled off the road, and into the ditch.

At breakfast, next morning, Richard was innocuously humorous on the subject of revolvers, burglars, and clairvoyant bulldogs. He was interrupted by a servant, who announced that Mr Hammond wished to speak to him for a moment.

"Right," said Richard. "Where is he?"

"He is just outside, sir," said the man. "Mr Hammond would not come in."

Hammond was a neighbour of Richard's, a robust and heavily built man. As a rule he was a cheerful sportsman, but this morning his countenance was troubled. His clothes were covered with dust, and he looked generally dishevelled.

"Hallo, Jim," said Richard cheerily. "How goes it? You look as if you'd been out all night."

"I have," said Hammond grimly. "So have several other men."

"Why? What's up?"

"Outbreak of rabies at Barker's farm. He shot one of the dogs, but the other got away. There must have been some damned mismanagement. A lot of us have been out trying to find the brute all night."

"But, by Jove, this is most awfully serious. Can't I help? I'm ready to start now if you like."

"Thanks, but I found the dog five minutes ago—dead in a ditch not twenty yards from your gate. He's there still."

"Who shot him?"

"Nobody. That's the trouble. He had been killed by another dog, as you'll see when you look at his windpipe. The chances are the other dog got bitten or scratched, and he'll carry on the infection. It's the other dog we've got to hunt."

"Could it be—" Richard paused.

"I'm afraid so," said Hammond. "Not many dogs would tackle a mad retriever, but your bulldog would. And it was close to your gate that the retriever was killed."

"If you'll wait half a minute, I'll see where Zero is."

But the dog was not to be found. Nobody had seen him that morning. In truth, Richard had not expected to find him. He left word that if the dog came back he was to be shut up in an empty stable. And then he and Hammond went out together.

"You've got a revolver, I suppose," said Richard.

"I don't hunt mad dogs without one. This is most awfully hard lines on you, Richard. He was a ripping good dog, Zero was."

"He was. It's Dick I'm thinking about. The dog was a great pal of his."

They found young Barker watching by the dead retriever. He explained gloomily that he had sent a boy for a cart. The body would be taken back and buried in lime. "And even then, sir, we've not got the dog that killed him."

"We're just going to get him," said Richard quietly.

They walked on in silence for a mile and then at a turn of the road they saw Zero, apparently asleep in the sunlight in the white dust.

"I ought to do this," said Richard, "but I wish you would."

"Right, old chap. It'll be over in a moment, and he'll be dead before he knows he's hurt. Look the other way."

"Richard turned round and waited, as it seemed to him, for a long time, waiting for the shot. Suddenly he heard Hammond's voice behind him.

"No need to shoot. The poor beggar's dead—been run over by a motor-car, I should say. It's a lucky accident."

"I wonder," said Richard.

"Wonder what?"

"Wonder if it was really an accident."

WHEN I WAS KING

I was in a part of the country where it is a good deal safer to kill a child than to take a pheasant. There are more people to look after the pheasants. I have always felt as if a man who could get his bird without a gun and cook it without a kitchen had a kind of right to the bird. An empty stomach is an argument too. Well, I got my bird, and then Bates got me. He is a big man and can use his hands. But all the same I am ready for him, man to man, at any time. He had three to help him that time, and that was why I had to stand up and look penitent while old White-whiskers talked nonsense before he sent me to prison.

I can talk the common talk, and I can talk like a gentleman by birth and education, which is what I happen to be. To Bates I gave the common talk—and very common some of it was. Just for a whim, to amuse myself, I gave the magistrate the other kind, knowing very well the sort of thing it would make him say.

"It is deplorable," said old White-whiskers, "that an evidently well-educated man like yourself, possessed of some abilities, and in a position to get your living by honest work, should take to this crime of poaching. The fact that you used violence towards the keeper makes the case all the worse. Men like you are a curse to the country."

Well, I have tried honest work. I have been a classical tutor. I have been an actor. I have been a bookmaker's clerk. But I like to go my own way at my own time. And that does not conduce to regular employment. My great-grandmother, I was always told, was a gipsy woman, and it may be that I have thrown back to her. I cannot say. I do know that I must go my own way at my own time, and that my own way is mostly out in the open, and that I do not love bricks and mortar.

It is not often that I stay for long in one place, and I had stayed too long in that village. There was a reason, of course, and if you guess that the reason was a woman, you need not trouble to guess again. I had a room at Mrs Crewe's cottage and paid my rent for it regularly. I had done very well with plovers' eggs earlier in the season, and had not spent all my money yet. It was a mistake to stop so long, because the keepers began to study me a little. They began to watch where I went and to ask themselves why. I had been marked by them long before I met Bates in the wood that night. They put me in prison, and it did not do me any good. It made me angry. I was a nice, well-conducted prisoner though, for the people who had to look after me had no responsibility in the matter. They did not make the laws, they were merely getting a living. I was principally angry with myself, because I had allowed another man to beat me. I made up my mind as soon as I got out of prison to take to the road again. I thought it would be better for my health if I could smell the air of a different county. It is a solemn fact that prison is not good for your health or strength. When I came out I was not the man that I had been.

And then I found out something which changed my mind. While I was in prison, Bates went after my girl and made love to her. That settled it. I had got to finish with Bates before I could go on.

I went to Mrs Crewe's cottage by night. When a man who has been in prison walks about in a small village in the daytime, remarks are likely to be made. If remarks were made, I was likely to take notice of them, and I did not want to get into trouble again. I made up my mind that Bates should be my next trouble. So, as I say, I went to Mrs Crewe by night, to do the fair thing by her. I told her that I must find a different room, if I had a room at all; for if old White-whiskers found that she was keeping the convicted poacher on, she would lose her cottage. "So, Mrs Crewe," I said, "I have come to say good-bye to you and Elsie."

Elsie is Mrs Crewe's little girl—a pretty kid of ten, but with bad health. It was not a good cottage for a sick child, and the food was not good enough for her, and the doctor was not good enough. He charged Mrs Crewe nothing—I'll say that for him—but it was as much as he was worth. Mrs Crewe's other daughter, Lizzie, was eight years older and in service in London.

Mrs Crewe heard all I had to say, but it made no effect upon her. She said that she had always paid her rent and conducted herself respectably, and that old White-whiskers dared not put her out, and that if he did put her out she would get somebody to write to the London newspapers about it. She had a great belief in the London newspapers. She said, moreover, that she took people as she found them, and that I had always treated her and Elsie well. That was true enough. If Elsie did not get that last pheasant, she had had others.

Mrs Crewe wanted, too, the money she would get from me for the room, and said so. She would take no money that she had not earned. She was that kind. She worked pretty hard too—sold the vegetables out of her bit of garden, did charing work whenever she could get it, and made a little out of her fowls. She said, too, that Elsie had not been so well, and had asked for me.

"Very well, Mrs Crewe," I said. "But there is one thing I have to tell you. I have been in prison, as you know, and something is going to happen which will put me back there again, and this time I shall not come out alive."

She said that she knew what I meant. Bates had not done the fair thing—that was acknowledged in the village. Still, I could do no good by getting violent again, and it was just as well that I should stop with her and let her talk me into a better frame of mind. I laughed. She was a good woman, but no amount of talk would have stopped me. And then I said I would sleep that night at her cottage.

I did, and nearly all night I heard that kid crying.

"What is the matter with Elsie?" I said.

Mrs Crewe told me. Lizzie had got permission to have Elsie up to London in the following week to see the King go past. Now the doctor had forbidden it. He was right too. She seemed to me to be pretty bad, and in the evening she was light-headed. I asked Mrs Crewe what she had done.

"Told her that as she can't go to London to see the King, I have written to Buckingham Palace to ask the King to come and see her. Anything to keep her quiet. Funny the way her mind is set on seeing the King."

"And why don't you write?" I asked. "If he knew, and if he could come, I believe he would."

"Aye," she said, "and so do I. But he might never see the letter, and kings have a deal to do, they tell me."

That day I tramped into Helmston to buy something that I wanted for Mr Bates, and as I walked into Helmston I could not get the thoughts of that kid out of my mind. Then a funny sort of idea struck me. I had been an actor, as I have already said, and I am pretty good at make-up. I bought a few other things in Helmston besides the revolver.

When I got back I told Mrs Crewe my idea, and at first she was opposed to it. She said that Elsie would be certain to recognise my face and voice, in spite of my disguise, and that if she found out she had been deceived, she would never forgive her.

"No," I said, "she will not recognise me. You yourself will not recognise me. I may not look very much like the King, but I shall not look in the least like myself. However, you yourself shall see first. If you think it is all right, as soon as it is dusk you shall go and tell her that the King has come."

I went to my room and spent about half an hour on that make-up. I think the result was pretty good, seeing that I had not got all the materials that I wanted to work with. I called Mrs Crewe up and she was astounded. She said now that it was perfectly safe, that nobody on earth could have recognised me.

"Very well," I said. "You must wait until ten minutes after the down-train is in. Elsie knows the trains and can hear them from where she is lying. You must tell her that the King does not wear his crown and his gorgeous robes when he is travelling, but only a black coat, just like the doctor."

When I was an actor I was never afflicted with nervousness; but as I heard Mrs Crewe in the next room tell Elsie exactly what I had told her to say, I shivered with fear. Suppose, after all, the child should find me out!

Elsie slept in a small bed in her mother's room. As I entered she tried to raise herself a little, and said in her best voice—the one that she used in church on Sunday—"I am so sorry that I cannot get up to make a curtsy to you. And ought I to call you 'Your Majesty' or just 'King'?"

"The correct etiquette," I said, "is for children to call me 'King'. I am very glad to have been able to come down to see you, Elsie. It was only by the merest chance that I could get away."

I gave her my whitened hand with the flash rings on it. She put her lips to it. "That will be something to tell the other girls," she said.

His Majesty inquired who the other girls were. He was told that Elsie had not been seeing much of them lately, because she had been ill; but she would be well and strong again very soon now—her mother had told her so. The other girls were very nice girls. Sarah Miggs had made a daisy-chain and sent it to her, and it was twice as long as the bed.

All this time Mrs Crewe had, by my direction, remained standing. She adopted a most respectful attitude, and curtsied whenever I looked at her. I now heard from her an ominous sniffling. If the silly woman began to blubber, there was a chance that the thing would be given away.

"Mrs Crewe," I said, with dignity, "you have our permission to retire."

She backed out of the room, and presently we heard her very busy in the kitchen, making an almost unnecessary noise with pots and pans. But perhaps that was intended to cover other sounds.

Elsie now demanded information about the interior of Buckingham Palace. I invented splendours, and she listened with rapture; she said it sounded more like Heaven than anything else. She put a plain question to me as to the value of the enormous diamond on my finger. She found that it had cost even more than she supposed, and she was interested in hearing the history of it. The diamond had once been the eye of an idol in India.

Presently she said, with distress: "Oh dear me, King, I do wish you could stop. There is such a lot more I want to ask you. But you will only just have time to catch the nine-thirteen, and that's the last up-train to-night."

"It is of no consequence," I said. "I had arranged to return to-night by motor-car."

"Shall I see it?"

"No," I said, "because by that time you will be asleep. It would not be a good thing for you to keep awake much longer. And if I tell you to go to sleep, then of course you must do it, because I am the King."

"Of course," she echoed. "Because you are the King."

But I could tell her all about the motor. It was really more like a house than a car. It had three rooms in it, and all the walls and ceilings were covered with a pattern of lilies made in silver and gold. The stalks and the leaves were silver and the flowers were gold. One of the rooms in the car was like a bedroom, and in one of the other rooms there was a cupboard which was entirely filled with glass jars of sweets. Elsie named several kinds; they were all there.

She held my hand as she talked, and she was still holding it as she fell asleep. The room was almost dark now, though outside it was a light night. Then quite suddenly she sat up in bed and flung wide her arms.

"God save the King!" she cried.

In a moment she was asleep again, and I slipped from the room. I was a king no longer. She slept well that night.

Old White-whiskers had his points after all. He took it into his head to have a look into his cottages himself, and in consequence a highly respectable firm lost a highly lucrative job. When Elsie and her mother get back from the seaside—White-whiskers is paying for them—they will find their cottage in decent repair.

And this morning I take the road again, never to return. Of course Mrs Crewe thinks that it is her wise counsel which has kept me out of the hands of the hangman; but that is not so.

I have not seen Bates again, and I have planned not to see him again, lest at the sight of him I should forget a decision to which I came when that kid of Mrs Crewe's sat up in bed and called upon God to save the King.

THE SATYR

Myra Larose was a good governess, capable, and highly certificated.

At Salston Hill School they rewarded her services with forty pounds per annum, and board and lodging during term-time. She had often been fortunate enough to secure private pupils for the holidays, and she knew a stationer who bought hand-painted Christmas cards. At the end of four years' work she had thirty-five pounds saved and in the Post Office. And then Aunt Jane, the last of her relatives, died, and left her a fine two hundred and fifty. This meant another ten pounds per annum.

Things were not so bad, but they did not, of course, justify the very mad idea that came into her pretty head—a head that, so far, had proved itself sane and practical.

The girls of the school considered that Miss Larose was strict but just, and that she had nice eyes. The principal, Mrs Dewlop, when prostrate from the horrible Davenant scandal, had declared that she would never think highly of any human being again; but she did think highly of Myra, even to the extent of considering the possibility of an increase of salary. Myra's fellow-teachers thought her sensible, and chaffed her mildly at times about her economies and her accumulation of wealth. No one would have supposed her capable of anything wild and extravagant.

Possibly a book that she had been reading put the idea into her head. Then there was the accident that nearly all her clothes were new simultaneously. Her eyes fell on the advertisement which showed her the advantages of hiring a petrol landaulet by the day in London. Thoughts of the theatre swam into her head. She loved the theatre, and had not been in one for years. She might lunch at the Ritz. She might deny herself nothing—for one day. Grey routine and miserable economies suddenly found her insurgent. Yes, she would have one great day—one day during which she would live at the rate of two thousand a year.

So, on one splendid morning, at the station of her northern suburb, she had occasion to be severe with the booking-clerk. ("I said *first* return—not third. You should pay more attention.") She bought a sixpenny periodical to read on the way up, and when she reached King's Cross she deliberately left the valuable magazine in the carriage behind her. That struck the high, reckless note. How often had she nursed a halfpenny paper through the whole of a traffic-distracted day that she might read the feuilleton at night!

"Taxi, miss?" suggested the porter when he had ascertained that she had no luggage.

"I think not," said Myra. "I believe my car's waiting for me." She felt that she had said it perfectly—without obvious pleasure, and without that air of intense languor that is always accepted on the stage as indicative of aristocracy, and never seen elsewhere.

She could tell the porter how to recognise the car—information supplied to her by the company from whom she had hired it—and the porter brought it up for her. Her first thought was that it looked splendid. Her second thought was that beyond a doubt she had recognised the face of the liveried driver.

She gave the porter a shilling, and sent him away. (Her usual tips for porters had varied from nothing to twopence, with a preference for the former.) Then she turned to the driver, a young man, with a handsome, clean-shaven face and dark, rebellious eyes.

"I know you," she said. "You are Mr Davenant."

"Quite true, Miss Larose. But that need make no difference. You have bought my services for the day, you know. You will find me just as attentive and respectful as any other servant. Where to, miss?"

"No, no. I want to talk to you. I must. Oh, it's too awful that you should have come down to this. Mrs Dewlop must have been vindictive indeed."

"She was certainly angry." He smiled reminiscently—he had a charming smile. "She had every right to be."

"Look here," she said impulsively, "what is to prevent you from lunching with me?"

"Your plans for the day—this car—and, for the matter of that, my clothes."

"I have no appointments, and no fixed plans. I was going to amuse myself just anyhow. I shall like this far better. Oh, can't you arrange it for me?"

"I should like it, too, and I can arrange it all very easily if you don't mind waiting half an hour."

"Of course I'll wait—wait here, if you like."

"You would find the National Gallery more interesting, and I can take you there in a few minutes."

"Yes, that's better. Thanks awfully. This is splendid."

At the National Gallery she looked at certain pictures with appreciative intelligence. Then she sat down and half-closed her eyes, and saw a picture from the gallery of her memory.

It was the big classroom at Salston Hill School. At one end of the room Myra Larose took the elementary class in drawing. At the other end, much older girls took the lesson in advanced drawing from a master who was, as the prospectus stated, an exhibitor at the Royal Academy. His name was Hilary Davenant, and in the bills he was charged extra. The older girls were ten in number, and were provided with easels, charcoal, and stumps. They formed the circumference of a circle of which the centre was a life-size cast with a blackboard adjacent.

Myra watched as she saw Davenant going from one drawing-board to another, and noted the waning of patience and the growth of irritation. He went to the blackboard and addressed the entire class on the anatomy of the hand, illustrating his remarks by rapid drawings on the blackboard. They were admirable drawings in their way—swift, right, certain, slick. And suddenly he flung the chalk to the floor and spake with his tongue. He also used gesture—a foreign and reprehensible practice.

"You poor, silly idiots! Not one of you will ever do it, except perhaps Miss Stenson. And if you did, it wouldn't be the real thing." He checked himself, and went on in a nice, suave schoolmaster's voice. "I was joking, of course. As I said, this cast presents considerable difficulties to some of you. But you must face your difficulties and overcome them. You must not let yourselves be discouraged." And so on.

Dora Stenson, aged sixteen, blushed and put her hand over her eyes. The other pupils smiled in a weak, wan way. They had been told that it was a joke, and they believed everything they were told, and did their best. At the other end of the room Myra Larose developed a good deal of interest in Hilary Davenant.

An incident which occurred two days later formed another picture in the memory-gallery. Myra, with other assistants, had been summoned with every circumstance of solemnity to the principal's private study.

"I have to inform you, ladies," said Mrs Dewlop, "that owing to circumstances which have come to my knowledge, I have been compelled to dismiss Mr H. Davenant at a moment's notice." She readjusted her pince-nez, and her refined face squirmed. "Mr Davenant is not a man: he is a satyr. I have sufficiently indicated the nature of his offence, which he admitted; and I do not care to dwell upon the subject further. This has been a great shock to me. One can only hope in time to live it down. That," she added tragically, "is all."

It had happened six months before, and at the time had filled Myra with curiosity and also with a touch of horror. Was it wise of her to make appointments with a man who had been so described? Had not her feeling of compassion for an old colleague—one, moreover, whom she had found sympathetic—carried her too far? This was not at all the kind of thing she had come out to do. But—well, she had done it. And if the satyr added punctuality to his other vices, he would be waiting outside for her.

He was there. He had changed his car as well as his clothes. He did not look poor. He looked as if he owned that car and a good deal of the rest of the earth.

"I hope you don't mind," he said. "I thought this open car might be useful. If you would be kind enough to take the seat beside me we could talk as we go. I thought, as it was such a ripping morning, you might like to drive into the country somewhere for lunch. But that must be just as you like, of course."

"It is exactly what I like. Let's see. We've got lots of time before lunch. You shall choose where we go."

"If you don't mind lunching a little late, we might do Brighton."

"Yes, we lunch at Brighton," she said decisively. The spirit of adventure was hot within her. She had meant the day to be rather exciting. It was more than fulfilling expectations.

As they crawled through the traffic she asked him how he had persuaded his firm to let her have the open car instead of the other. She was told that it was the policy of his people to oblige a customer in every possible way, and that they had made no trouble. Then she spoke of things she had seen at the National Gallery, and found him just as enthusiastic about art as she had done once in the old days at the school, when chance gave them a few minutes' talk together. But it was not till they sat at lunch in a good little hotel overlooking the sea that they became confidential.

"I gather," he said, "that you knew that Mrs Dewlop sacked me."

"She told all of us."

"Did she say why?"

"Not exactly. She said that you were a satyr. I—I didn't believe that."

"Well, I'll tell you exactly what I did. I kissed Dora Stenson."

This was a blow. "I don't think I want to hear about it," said Myra coldly.

"It's all very well," said Davenant mournfully, "but I'd had very little experience as a teacher. What do you do yourself when a girl begins to cry?"

"If she's quite a child, I try to comfort her. If it's one of the older girls, I tell her that I dislike hysteria, and that she had better go away until she has recovered. But it rarely happens with the older girls. What made Dora Stenson cry?"

"All my own fault—the whole thing. You know the beauties I had to teach. Dora was the only one that had any gift. As for the rest, you might as well have tried to teach blind pigs to draw. What was the consequence? I gave Dora most of the teaching, and I was harder on her than I was on the others. I judged her by a different standard, and I drove her as hard as I could. Well, one day, at the end of the hour, she brought me up some bad work. She'd taken no trouble. It was rotten. All the same, if any of the others had shown me anything nearly as good, I should have been more than satisfied. As it was Dora, I lost my wool and told her what I thought. Classes were dismissed. You went out. I was left alone in the room. Back came Dora to pick up some truck she'd left behind, and she was crying—crying like anything. Well, I couldn't stand it. I'd never meant to be a brute, and there was that girl—very pretty she is, too—crying like anything. I began to talk to her, and, before I knew where I was, I had kissed her. I'm making a clean breast of the whole thing—I kissed her two or three times."

Miss Myra Larose, who had not wanted to hear about it, had listened with breathless interest, and now put in a shrewd question.

"And did Dora kiss you?"

"As I was saying, where I was wrong was in—"

"All right, I know. If she had not kissed you, you would have said so. But, seeing that she did kiss you, why on earth did she complain to Mrs Dewlop?"

"She never did. She wrote a letter to a girl friend of hers, and left it lying about. Mrs Dewlop read it. Now, what do you think?"

Myra considered a moment. "I think," she said deliberately, "that Dora was a braggart, and that Mrs Dewlop was a sneak, and—er—not very wise, and that you——"

"Do you also think me a satyr?"

"Of course not. You were all wrong, but you were just a baby."

He gave a sigh of relief.

"It makes me angry," said Myra impulsively. "What right had that woman to ruin you, and turn you into a cab-driver?"

"I must explain further. It is true that she refused me any kind of a character, and that my teaching career was closed. But I am not exactly a cab-driver. When I was turned out I had to give up the idea of making a living by art. I could no longer teach, and modern pictures sell seldom and badly. But I had another string to my bow. I understand motors, and I had had plenty of driving experience. An uncle of mine is in the motor business to some considerable extent. Amongst other things, he is a director and principal share-holder in the company from which you hired your car. He has often asked me to join him, and now I did so. He is a thorough sort of man, and he insisted that I should go through every side. I've washed cars; for three months I was an ordinary mechanic; I've been in the office; the last few weeks I've been driving these privately let cars, and picking up some interesting information as to the amount of tips that the drivers get. Next week I shall be a manager. Well, now, I saw your order when it came in. I remembered you very well—very well, indeed. I determined to drive you myself—to be your good servant, if that was all that was possible, but to be as much more as you would let me be."

As the car purred smoothly through the dusk in the direction of the northern suburb where Myra had her inexpensive lodging, Davenant said: "Then you will give notice that you leave at the end of next term, darling?"

And she said: "Yes, dearest."

THE CHOICE

Mrs Halward, a good and earnest lady, was angry with her married brother, Harry Elton, and took an early opportunity of telling him so. Elton was a big man, and so quiet as to be almost gloomy.

"What are you angry for?" he asked.

"You know perfectly well. It's shameful. It's scandalous. I can't think how you can do it. You've only been married six years, and Grace is such a dear."

"Yes," said Elton, "I'm very fond of Grace."

"I was under the impression," said his sister, "that you were very fond of Rosamond Fayre. It has been sufficiently obvious lately."

"Yes," said Elton slowly, "I'm extremely fond of Rosamond."

"Don't talk like a fool. A man can't be in love with two women at the same time."

"If he can't, why accuse me of it? Has Grace complained to you?"

"Of course not. Have you been married to her for six years without discovering that she has a certain amount of pride?"

"Because, you see, if she has not complained to you, I don't see how it becomes your business at all. I am sure it is not a thing you would understand. You mean well, of course; but interference is futile. A man neither loves nor ceases to love because he is told it is expected of him, and that the conventions require it. You women who try to direct the love-affairs of others always remind me of a certain king who forbade the tide to come in."

"I have done my duty," said his sister stoutly. "You are going to bring disgrace on the family. I shall certainly speak to Grace about it."

"Do, if you wish. I warn you that Grace is not so patient as I am. If you succeed you will make mischief. You will precipitate things. That's curious, you know—the third party who interferes with the relations between a man and a woman can never do any good, but is able to do a deal of harm."

Mrs Halward was not convinced. If her sister-in-law had been at home at the time she would probably have spoken to her then. She could only repeat that she had done her duty, and leave with dignity.

Mrs Fayre was extremely poor. Her husband held a position in China, vaguely understood to be mercantile, and sent her one hundred pounds a year. In addition to this she had a private income of seven hundred; but eight hundred a year is extreme poverty when most of your friends and acquaintances approximate to eight thousand a year. She lived in a small flat in South Kensington, and made a business of pathos. At one time, Mrs Halward had been enchanted with her, and it was at her house that Rosamond and Harry Elton first met.

Harry Elton walked up and down the library, and tried to think things out. He thought Rosamond beautiful. He liked the tone of her voice. He liked her to be with him. Once or twice he had nearly kissed her, but he never had kissed her, and he had never told her he loved her. There were times when he had been on the verge of it, but had been checked by the thought that he could not do Grace any wrong—not only because it would hurt her, but because it would hurt himself. What was the use of laying down stupid rules, that a man could not love two women at once? But the rule had been laid down, and it was almost universally accepted. If a man did love two women, it was certain that each of the women would feel herself wronged.

He had never wanted to face the situation at all. He had been quite willing to let things drift. His wife was not jealous. He saw Rosamond Fayre frequently, and without any secrecy. He had interested himself in her painting—which was abominable—and had tried to get her work. Sometimes they lunched or dined at a restaurant alone together. Sometimes he took her to the theatre. But he had never realised that he had given the thing away, and that the cats—among whom he included his sister—had marked him down. Now that he did face the situation, he did not in the least know what to do. He thought of leaving Grace and of running away with Rosamond, and the thought was intolerable. He thought of giving up Rosamond by degrees, seeing less and less of her, and that thought was equally intolerable. He planned to let things remain as they were, and recognised that *that* was impossible. No love-affair remains at a fixed point half-way. It goes on and on.

He stepped over to the telephone at his desk and contemplated it for a few seconds, as if he were seeking counsel from it. Then he took down the receiver and asked for a number.

"That is you, Rosamond?"

"Quite."

"I've been thinking about you."

"I've been thinking about you, too."

"I want you to tell me something. Do you think that I love you?"

"Oh, yes, of course." The tone of the voice was mocking.

"I am serious," said Elton.

There were a few seconds of silence. What had happened?

"Are you there?" he asked.

"It is very dangerous to be serious. Good-bye."

"You have not been sleeping well lately, have you?" Grace asked her husband.

"Oh yes," he lied. "What makes you think that?"

"Well, you look horribly tired, anyhow. I don't believe you're well. I do wish you'd see a doctor."

Harry reassured her. He was, he said, as fit as could be.

"Well, what are you and Rosamond Fayre going to do after dinner?"

"Don't know exactly. It depends upon what she wants. A theatre, I suppose. Is there anything going on not too absolutely rotten?"

"Nothing that I have seen lately. If you can get out of it, don't take her to the theatre. Get home early and go to bed. You really look as if you wanted a rest."

Grace was going to hear Kubelik that evening, dining first with the Halwards. Her husband did not hear Kubeliks cheerfully, and it had been Grace's suggestion that he should take poor Rosamond to dine somewhere. Everyone felt they must do something for poor Rosamond to get a little colour and brightness into her days. Eight hundred a year and a husband in China! What a life!

Harry Elton had accepted the suggestion without enthusiasm. He said he supposed he might as well do that as anything else.

It was part of the tragedy of Rosamond's poverty that she could not afford as many taxicabs as she needed. She went about a good deal, and she found it necessary to go about economically. Left to herself, she would have taken the tube to Dover Street and then stepped across the road. But Elton's expensive motor-car, after taking Grace to the Halwards', went on to South Kensington to fetch Rosamond.

She was grateful, as she always was. "I often wonder," she said plaintively, "why everybody is so good to me—you especially."

"I am by no means certain that I am good to you. I spoke to you on the telephone this afternoon."

"Not now, no," said Rosamond firmly.

She was quite right. You cannot discuss the sweet and secret sinfulness of your heart when the waiter is handing you the entrée. Possibly Elton also recognised this. But his next remark was rather brutal.

"You have never told me about the man in China. Tell me now."

Rosamond answered in French. There were no waiters near at the moment to overhear her. If there had been, they all understood French perfectly. But to Rosamond, French had always given a feeling of security. Her story was brief and simple. She had married at eighteen. It had been a girl's infatuation, and it had lasted just two years. No, there had never been any actual break between them. He had to take up this post in China. They were too poor for him to refuse it. It brought him five hundred a year.

"Out of which," said Elton, "he sends you a measly hundred."

"He knows I have some means of my own. Oh no, we have never quarrelled. It is just that the thing died. I should be sorry for his death, as I should be for the death of any old companion—nothing more than that. He would regard my death in the same way. There is no longer any love between us. He sends me four rather formal letters every year, and I send him four replies, telling him about London theatres and so on. It's funny, isn't it? But, my God!" (It did not sound so strong in French.)

"I do not think," said Elton slowly, "that you were meant to spend your years without love."

"No? How do you know?"

Elton smiled. "Do you know the eyes of women who do without love and do not need it? They are the eyes of a business-like fish. Your eyes are not like that."

She leant a little forward over the small table. "Look into them," she said, "and tell me what you read there."

"Don't do that. Do you want to drive me mad?"

"Yes—sometimes."

"Well, I dare not tell you what I read in your eyes."

She laughed nervously. "Is it so bad as that?" she said, and began to speak of other matters.

She was intending to send a picture to the Academy, and felt quite hopeful about it. She described it to him, and he made appropriate replies; but though he watched her intently all the time he was hardly conscious of what she was saying. He tried to pull himself together.

"What are we to do this evening? A theatre?"

"I don't think so. I'm tired of theatres. I'm tired of everything. We will talk for a little in the lounge, and then I will take my train back again and go through the farce of trying to go to sleep."

"You, too, have not been sleeping well then? Of course, you won't go back in the train. I shall drive you back."

"It is frightfully good of you, but I don't really deserve so much kindness to-night. I have the feeling all the time that I am behaving badly, and talking like an idiot."

"Come on into the lounge. We will both talk like idiots."

They found a secluded corner, and a waiter brought them coffee. Elton watched the man's back as he went away. Then he turned to Rosamond.

"Now then," he said, "about our conversation on the telephone."

She paused before replying, breathing quickly, and then she spoke very rapidly and in a low voice.

"Yes, you love me. I have known that for a long time. I wanted you to love me. You know the rest, don't you? I adore you. There's no one but you in the world. Now I've said it. It was bound to happen sooner or later. It's over, and we can never speak to one another again."

He rose from his place. "Come," he said, "I am going to take you home. I had the car waiting here in case we wanted to go to the theatre."

He signed to a waiter.

"Go and find my car, Mr Elton's car," he said to the man, "and tell the driver he won't be wanted to-night. He is to go home."

Rosamond looked at him wonderingly. "I—I think I see."

"Of course. Get your cloak quickly, dear."

He put her into the taxi and gave the address, not of the little flat where she lived, but of her studio.

"Things are better," said Mrs Halward to her husband. "I was afraid at one time that there was going to be serious trouble between Harry and his wife about that wretched Fayre. I gave him a word of warning at the time, and I am convinced it did good."

"What makes you think so?" said her husband, not greatly interested.

"Didn't you notice yourself at dinner last night? He hardly said five words to Rosamond. He seemed to take no notice of her."

Mrs Halward had observed correctly, but had made wrong deductions. Harry and Rosamond were meeting more frequently than ever, but nearly always in secrecy. If his wife suggested that Rosamond should be asked to one of her dinner-parties, Harry shrugged his shoulders and made some excuse. He lunched frequently at his club now, so his wife said, and she said what he had told her. As a matter of fact, he never lunched there at all. He took Rosamond to out-of-the-way restaurants where he would be unlikely to meet anybody he knew. Sometimes they improvised a lunch in the studio together. No day passed that he did not see her, or, at any rate, hear from her. And there was no happiness for either of them. Elton hated lies and hated secrecy. Grace had never been jealous of Rosamond, but Rosamond was furiously jealous of Grace.

"I can see the end of this," said Rosamond one night when he had come late to the studio. "We cannot possibly go on like this. It is killing me. I cannot share you with another woman."

"I know, dear," said Elton. "The position is hateful. And it is all my fault. And what is to be the end of it?"

"Quite simple," said Rosamond. "I take something for my insomnia, you know. There will be an accident."

"You are not to say that, and you are not even to think about it. That will not be the end. I am going to take you away. We must face it. A little scandal, a change of name, and, in a year, it is all over. I shall be willing enough to live abroad. We will go to your beloved Sicily."

"Yes, to Taormina. Oh! but that would be too much happiness. That could never be."

But, there and then, they made their plans how it should be.

Even now, if there was a prospect of happiness for Rosamond, there seemed to Elton to be none for himself. He would have to leave Grace. It was against accepted ideas and against rules, but, none the less, he loved Grace. He could not have said which woman he loved more—Grace or Rosamond. They were so absolutely different—Grace with her suavity and Rosamond with her temperament—that no comparison was possible. Both seemed absolutely necessary to him, and he could not have both.

Grace and her husband had to fulfil an engagement to spend a week-end with some friends who lived in Oxfordshire. One morning she went out alone and found the cottage of her dreams—the country cottage she had always meant to have. She came back in the spirits of a child who has a new toy. Harry was to go and look at it at once.

"And what do you think I have done? I have telegraphed to that poor Rosamond Fayre to come down here on Monday morning. I am going to give her a commission—to paint my cottage garden. She is rather good at gardens—I mean she is better at gardens."

It was useless to raise any objection, and Harry felt convinced Rosamond would not come. So he said it was rather a good idea, and discussed gravely the improvements his wife meant to make at the cottage.

"You see," she said, "I must make it comfortable."

A little later the telegram arrived from Rosamond: "Very many thanks. Will come by the train you suggest."

Harry met that train at his wife's suggestion.

"Why did you come?" he asked Rosamond anxiously.

"Didn't you want to see me?"

"I always want to see you, but the position is too horrible."

"I know it is difficult, but in three days now it will all be over, and we shall be at peace together. Meanwhile, if I refuse to meet Grace, she will think—oh, she may think anything. Come on. Take me to the cottage."

Harry made an excuse to leave the two women alone there together. He would be back in an hour. And in a little more than an hour he was walking back to the station with Rosamond and his wife. There was only just time to catch Rosamond's train. But it was all right, so Grace said; there was a short cut across the line. They would be there in time. And then Grace made a terrible discovery. She had left the key of the cottage in the door. Harry must run back and fetch it, or the people who were letting her the cottage would consider she was not a responsible person.

Harry tried the door of the cottage to see that it was locked, put the key in his pocket, and ran after them. They had reached the crossing now, but were standing still. He could not at first make out what it was they were doing. Rosamond then bent down to her shoe, and Harry realised what had happened. The shoe had got wedged in the points, and she would have to take her foot out of it to get free.

And then he heard the scream of the whistle, and dashed forward.

He managed to save one of the two women. It was Grace.

The moment had revealed him to himself. He had made his choice.

THE PIANO-TUNER

CHAPTER I

Miss Caterham was forty-five, and said so, and looked it. She wore black cashmere in the afternoon, and black silk in the evening. She was methodical, and professed a hatred of all nonsense. She liked to take care of everything and to avoid using it. Also, though fundamentally kind-hearted, she was firm even to the point of obstinacy. Her ideas were old-fashioned, and she had only hatred and contempt for any other ideas. She kept fowls and understood them completely. She also kept her orphan niece, Ruth Caterham, and understood her less completely. Indisputably she loved the fowls much less than she loved her niece, but the fowls had comparatively the greater liberty. She maintained a decent, upper-middle-class state in a Georgian house, on the confines of a little town that thoroughly respected her. It was not a suburb. It was too far from London for that. The best trains took forty minutes. Miss Caterham was rather acidulated about suburban people.

There, from time to time, she entertained the brother of Ruth's deceased mother. She loved him, and abhorred his opinions. So far as might be, she kept him in order. His name was George Maniways, and he was in Parliament, and his politics were of the wrong colour. "You and the other enemies of England," Miss Caterham would say, in addressing him. She would probably have quarrelled with him, frequently, but for the fact that it takes two to make a quarrel, and Mr Maniways was too lazy to play up properly. His temper was so good as to be almost pusillanimous. He was almost the only male who ever entered her house, except in a menial capacity. She had been compelled to allow Ruth to accept the Sotherings' dance and Lady Rochisen's. But when young Bruce Sothering wrote to ask if he might call, she replied that they were just going away, but that she would write on her return. She did not write on her return. And she cannot have forgotten it, for Ruth reminded her twice. Rather a difficult woman, Miss Caterham.

The day being hot, George had arrayed his long and meagre body in white flannel. The conformation of his large grey moustache and his apologetic blue eyes gave him the appearance of rather a meek kind of walrus—one that would feed from the hand and do trust-and-paid-for. He reposed himself after luncheon in a large deck-chair on the veranda. He held between his teeth an amber tube with a cigarette in it. He had a box of matches in one hand, and intended to light the cigarette when he felt more rested. In the meantime he nursed a straw hat, and watched Miss Caterham's wise and just restraint of a climbing geranium. Miss Caterham, in the intervals of her work, watched George, with a glance which indicated rapidly increasing displeasure. The fire kindled, and at last she spake with her tongue.

"I am extremely sorry, George, but I simply cannot stand it any longer. Will you kindly either light that cigarette or throw it away."

"I was just about to light it, Jane. This weather, especially after luncheon, invests one's actions with a certain amount of deliberation."

"If you showed as much deliberation about your words, George, as you do about your actions, it would be better for everybody."

George's astonishment was such that he let out the match which he had just lit. "Oh, really, Jane, I wasn't conscious of having said anything particular."

"It's not what you said now, it's what you said at luncheon. If you don't strike another match and light that cigarette, I shall have to go."

George followed his instructions obediently. "At luncheon?" he said meditatively. "Don't seem to remember having said anything particular at luncheon either. While I'm here, I'm always careful to avoid politics."

"So long as you follow blindly the foes of your own country, that is just as well. The treacherous and unpatriotic duffers, with whom you have chosen to ally yourself——"

"Yes," said George. "You're perfectly right. It's much better to avoid politics. But what did I say at luncheon?"

"Ruth was there."

"She was. Very charming she looked. I'm proud to be her uncle."

"I have the charge of her education, and the formation of her moral character, and I considered what you said to be most unwise. Praise is nearly always bad, and it is specially injudicious to praise a child's beauty to her face."

"Oh, that's it, is it? Well, Ruth ain't exactly a child, you know. She's eighteen."

"Only just eighteen, and I'm not sure that that does not make it worse. I've always been careful to guard against anything of the kind. I do not wish my niece to grow up vain and self-conscious."

"Oh, she's all right," said George feebly.

"Far from it. She is wilful, and there is nothing I hate so much as wilfulness. I must have my own way, and I cannot be opposed in my views by you or by Ruth. Also, it is quite untrue that she is beautiful. She is nice-looking enough, but her mouth is certainly a little too large, and she has permitted the sun to ruin her complexion—in spite of my advice. I must request you, George, to abstain from saying anything of the kind again."

George refused an invitation to inspect a new fowl-run, and said that he preferred to sit and think over things. Amongst other thoughts, it occurred to him that his niece did not in all probability have much of a time. Where he sat, he could hear faintly the sound of the piano in the drawing-room. It was obviously something of Grieg's, and appallingly difficult. He was glad that he had not got to play it, and was merely an audience. He had chosen the better part. After all, Ruth had her music to occupy her, and she played tennis with the Vicarage girls, and what else could she want? He was just dropping off to sleep when the cessation of the music roused him again. A moment later his niece stood before him.

She was a tall girl, and carried herself well. Most people would have agreed with her uncle's estimation of her looks. She wore no hat, and her face was certainly slightly tanned.

"Uncle George," she said, "I want you to do something."

"Not tennis," said George sleepily. "Nothing violent. After tea, perhaps, when it's cooler."

"That's not it at all. Now listen. When you're at the House, you have tea on the Terrace sometimes, don't you?"

"Sometimes. Whisky-and-soda sometimes. What do you want?"

"You can ask people to come and have tea on the Terrace, can't you? Well, you've got to ask me. Next Tuesday, please. And you've got to persuade Aunt Jane to let me go, too."

"I'm not so sure about that," said George. "I've just been getting into a row about you. I'm not at all sure that I'm not a bad influence, and that any proposal of mine would not be vetoed."

"You can do it all right," said the girl decisively, "if you go the right way about it. Say that it's historical. I mean that your silly old House of Commons is historical. It would have a great educational value for me. You could show me where Chatham stood when he made his last grand speech, and fell down in the middle of it."

"That happened to be in another place, to wit, the House of Lords."

"It's all the same. And rub it in a bit about Burke—she's keen on Burke. Keep up a good strong educational line, and Aunt Jane will be glad to let me go."

"Very well. I'll do what I can. Next Tuesday at four o'clock. Tell me what time your train gets to Euston, and I'll meet it."

Ruth looked away from him, and appeared to be addressing one of the pillars of the veranda. "I don't think you need meet it. In fact, I'd rather you didn't. I know my way about London very well. You just wait at the House of Commons. And if I'm not there by a quarter past four, don't worry. It will only mean that I've changed my mind and gone somewhere else."

George whistled. "Well I never," he said. "And what might you be up to?"

"I'd much rather you didn't ask about it."

"Well, at any rate, who is he?"

George did not in the least suppose that there was any "he" in the case, and was rather surprised that Ruth blushed.

"There," said Ruth, "I told you not to ask. Now I suppose you won't do it."

"Reverting to the original question, who is he?"

"Well, you've always said that all men are equal, haven't you?"

"In one sense, yes. All men are not equally desirable as companions for my niece."

"He is the man who came to tune the piano last week. You always said class distinctions were all rot. We are going to see some pictures together, and then he's going to give me tea—at least, he was. But now I suppose you won't let us, though he's quite nice really. But at any rate you'll have to promise not to sneak about it to Aunt Jane."

"Promise for promise. Will you promise not to marry a piano-tuner?"

Ruth burst out laughing. "Rather," she said. "Absolutely."

CHAPTER II

Like most lazy and good-tempered men, George could show a good deal of energy and decision, when the occasion arose. He began work that night, after Ruth had gone up to bed.

"You're not such a careful housekeeper as you used to be, Jane."

This was quite untrue, and he knew it to be untrue. He also knew that it would make Jane angry.

"Perhaps," she said, "you will tell me, George, what prompts you to make such a perfectly senseless remark. One of the glasses on the dinner-table to-night was not properly polished. I have already spoken about it. But I'm quite positive you never noticed it."

"No," said George. "I noticed that your piano was out of tune. Why don't you have it done regularly?"

"Everything in this house is done regularly. The piano is tuned once every three months. In this case you're more particularly in the wrong, because it had an extra tuning last week. Ruth thought it wanted it, and wrote to Brinswoods to send a man."

"That man ought to get the sack," said George with confidence. "What was his name?"

"My dear George, how on earth should I know? Piano-tuners don't have names. They have sherry and a biscuit. They are just the piano-tuner. It was Ruth who showed him what was required—I never even saw him. And she was quite satisfied with what he had done. I think you must own that Ruth is a better judge in musical questions than yourself."

"Very likely," said George, and changed the subject. The newspaper provided him with a topic. A young lady had just eloped with her father's chauffeur. A young lady, moreover, who had been most strictly brought up. He remembered other instances. Miss Caterham seemed uneasy.

"But Ruth is not in the least like that," she said.

"Of course not. Who's thinking about Ruth? Besides, she's not brought up in that silly way. She sees plenty of society, plenty of young men of her own class, and is not likely to make a mistake."

"Ruth has been brought up with the greatest care, and I hope with wisdom. Where you go so wrong about Ruth, George, is in regarding her as a mere child. She is eighteen. You are inclined to forget that."

George took the rebuke meekly. Miss Caterham continued: "I have always been intending to make some slight changes in view of her age. She has already been to two dances."

"You don't want to overdo it," said the subtile George. "You needn't be in the least nervous about Ruth."

Before returning to London next day, George had a few moments of serious conversation with Ruth. At least, George was perfectly serious. Ruth rather presented the appearance of an amused person with a secret. Her Uncle George gave her six invitations, and she accepted all of them.

"But will Aunt Jane stand it?" she asked.

"I think," said George, "that your aunt will make no difficulties."

Ruth went to tea on the Terrace. Ruth went to theatres and concerts. On three occasions she met Mr Bruce Sothering.

And when, a few days later, she announced her engagement to Mr Bruce Sothering, she met with the heartiest congratulations from her uncle, and with no serious opposition from her aunt. And in the ordinary course of events, Mr Bruce Sothering came to see Miss Caterham.

Miss Caterham would have been interested if she could have heard what they said about it in the kitchen.

"I'm making no mistake at all," said the parlour-maid. "I don't care how rich he is or how well connected. That Mr Bruce Sothering is the young man who came to tune the piano last time. It's not a question of a likeness."

"But why?" said the cook.

"Hintrigue," said the butler darkly.

THE PEARLS AND THE SWINE

Miss Markham in certain respects was a fortunate lady. She had a flat in town and had recently acquired a little bungalow for week-end purposes on a cliff that overlooked the sea. There are one or two other little bungalows in the vicinity, and the people who own them do not give away the name of the place; they fear the penalties of popularity.

Miss Markham had sufficient means and no worries; she was good-looking enough for all practical purposes. She was forty-five years of age, had never been engaged, had never even come within a mile of being engaged.

In her London flat Miss Markham was quite conventional, and kept the usual servants; in the sacred privacy of her bungalow by the sea, she kept no regular servants at all. An old woman who lived in the village was paid to keep an eye on the place while Miss Markham was away, though no one could have said precisely what good it had done the place to have an eye kept there. The same old woman, when Miss Markham grew tired of town and came down for the week-end, spent the day at the bungalow, and—to use her own expression, which is not to be taken literally—"did for her".

July in London was very hot that year. Miss Byles said that she would only be too delighted to go down to the bungalow, at the place which may not be mentioned, in company with Miss Markham. At the last moment Miss Byles was compelled, by health, to break her engagement. She did everything at the wrong time; she got hay fever at the wrong time; therefore Miss Markham went down alone, and the old woman made some perfunctory preparations for her, cooked an alleged dinner for her, and made no secret of the fact that she regarded it as a grievance that she should have to do anything whatever in return for the money which she received.

Having done as little as possible, she returned, so to speak, to her nest, and Miss Markham was left absolutely alone in the bungalow.

At ten o'clock that night Miss Markham, who was almost excessively refined, had just put down her copy of Walter Pater's "Imaginary Portraits", and was thinking of crossing the passage to go to bed. At that moment, her attention was attracted by a gentle tap on her front door: it was not the urgent, sharp, business tap of the Post Office; it was the rippling, social tap. Miss Markham was not nervous; she looked out of the window before deciding to open the door. Even with the moon to help her she could see nothing very distinctly, but it was obviously a man who was standing there, and he appeared to be a well-dressed man. She at once decided that he was a guest on his way to one of the other bungalows, and that he had called on her by mistake. Having come to this totally erroneous conclusion, she opened the door.

The visitor stood in the light now, and there was nothing about him to cause her perturbation. He was a tall man, about thirty years of age, with a short yellow beard and trustful, melancholy blue eyes. He wore a grey lounge suit and patent leather shoes, and he carried in his hand a very small brown bag.

"Miss Markham?" he said, raising his hat.

"I am Miss Markham."

"I really must apologise for disturbing you at this time of night. The fact of the case is that you live in a lonely spot; I wish to inquire if you are insured against burglary."

Miss Markham was rather amused by the impertinence of him. It was all very well for an insurance-office tout to call upon her to get her to take out a policy, but it did seem a little bit too much that he should call at so late an hour. If Miss Markham had not liked the man's appearance, she would have been even more severe than she was.

"I am afraid," she said, "that you have troubled yourself, and incidentally have troubled me, to no purpose. I am already insured against burglary, fire, employers' liabilities, and all the rest of it, and I am not proposing to take out any further policy."

"I am so glad," said the stranger, and in a flash stepped into the hall, and shut the door behind him.

"What are you doing?" said Miss Markham. "You must not come in here like that. Go away at once!"

"I know, my dear lady, it is quite unconventional and wrong, and I can only assure you if you had not been insured against burglary I should never have come in. You may believe me that in the exercise of my profession, I have always done my best to consult the feelings of others."

"Your profession! What profession?"

"We won't give it a name. 'What's in a name?' Some of my confrères are rough and violent; I am nothing of the kind. Naturally if you began to make a noise, I should have to take some steps to prevent it. The police in this neighbourhood are few in number and quite inefficient, and I think there is no other bungalow within a quarter of a mile."

Miss Markham was now alive to the state of the case.

"I think," she said, "that a police-whistle can be heard at that distance."

She raised her police-whistle just as he raised his revolver; the two hands went up together.

"Really, Miss Markham, you ought not to force me into such a totally false position. My feelings towards you are those of a chivalrous gentleman; it absolutely repels me to do anything whatever which would appear in the nature of a threat. You have put the police-whistle down? That's right. Now then we can talk about this necklace. It would be pleasanter if we sat down; we will go into the dining-room, shall we? I say the dining-room rather than the drawing-room, because I think you might possibly like to ask me to take a whisky-and-soda, and the decanters are there."

Miss Markham followed him into the dining-room; she did not ask him to take a whisky-and-soda. Notwithstanding this, he took it.

"Tell me one thing," she said, "how did you know about this necklace?"

"That is just it; servants will talk. They are an eternal nuisance, aren't they? If their employer has anything which is believed to be valuable, they like to brag about it a little. You know, one can understand it; they enjoy reflected glory. It is exactly twelve months ago since I learned in casual conversation with a lady of inferior station to myself—your housemaid, I believe—that you not only possessed a pearl necklace valued at £500, but that you always wore it."

"The jeweller told me that pearls should always be worn; they keep their colour better that way."

"Yes," said the stranger, "they do give that advice; very useful advice it is too."

"If there is nothing else that you want to take," said Miss Markham, "perhaps you would not mind going."

"Certainly, my dear lady. I understand your point of view exactly. Here we have an abominable intrusion at a late hour; my sex makes the intrusion all the worse. When you are about to summon assistance, I raise my revolver, and if you had not put the police-whistle down, I should have been reluctantly compelled to shoot you dead. I then take away from you, as I shall do presently, a pearl necklace, which you value at £500, though I shall be quite satisfied if I get £120 for it myself. Well, when you come to think of it, you must admit that you have suffered nothing but a little inconvenience. The insurance company will give you £500 to buy another necklace, and the one which I am about to take away with me has no sentimental associations for you."

"How do you know that?"

"You bought the silly thing yourself; correct me if I am wrong."

She did not correct him. She said, "I don't see how you know."

"Ah!" said the burglar, "there we come to another point—my point of view; we have had yours, but you have not had mine. I wonder if it would interest you to hear it? It might possibly, simply on the score of novelty. One hears a very great deal about the feelings of the householder towards the burglar, but precious little of the feelings of the burglar towards the householder; and I am not even a common burglar, as I hope you have recognised. It might interest you to talk the thing over for a few minutes, and it would be a great privilege and pleasure to myself. It might not, and in that case I will leave you at once."

Miss Markham hesitated. Then she took a chair by the table and sat down.

"Well," she said, "I will hear what you have to say."

"I have never seen you before to-night. I opened the door and you stood in the light. In the background were the white walls of the bungalow and on them good mezzotints after the eighteenth-century masters, and on a small rosewood table was your bedroom candlestick—Sheffield, and I should say a very good piece; good Sheffield, as you know, fetches more than silver nowadays. But it was upon you principally that my attention was centred. The rest all came in a flash; your grey quaker dress, the green serge curtains, the copper knocker, everything told the same story of simplicity and taste. But in your face I read very much more, so much that was not simple, so much that still perplexes me."

Miss Markham was slightly embarrassed. It was not usual for her to hear herself discussed. One part of her said this was monumental impertinence, and she must check it. The other part said that she rather liked it. It was the other part of her that won. If he had not been an unusually handsome man, with melancholy blue eyes and a beautiful respectful manner, perhaps the other part would have won.

She laughed. "I do not see what there is to puzzle you."

"I saw the face of a saint. You have lived absolutely apart from the world; in a walled-in garden as it were. Now I personally have all the vices." He took from his pocket a gold cigarette case with another man's monogram on it, took out a cigarette and lit it. "As I was saying, I have all the vices, but that does not mean that I am without a very keen appreciation of the other thing; perhaps the keener, because I have not got it. I have seen faces like yours before, but they have always belonged to someone who wore the garb of a nun. The nuns shut out the world from them; you, on the contrary, have lived in the world, and have still kept apart from it. I cannot make out how you have done it. I cannot make out how you have been allowed to do it. Tell me, has no man ever kissed you?"

"Never," she said fervently.

"I believe you," said the burglar. "I think I have never met another woman in whom I would have believed a similar declaration. You will observe that I did not offer you a cigarette, because I knew for a fact that you have never smoked."

"Never," she said.

"I knew it; just as I knew that you had bought this pearl necklace yourself; just as I knew that you had never been kissed; just as I knew that you were good enough to compel even the abject reverence of as bad a man as myself."

Her hand, toying nervously with things on the table, happened to strike the decanter. "But won't you have some more of this?" she said.

He glanced at a gold watch, on the back of which another man's armorial bearings were engraved. "I have only two minutes," he said, "but I must drink your health at parting. Do you know that it is absolutely right for you to wear pearls? Coloured stones would be quite wrong; diamonds are too hard; pearls give just the right note of purity and softness. I suppose you have realised that with the exception of one ring, you wear no other gems. I noticed that ring as I came in. Those large table-cut emeralds, when they are of that fine quality, fetch a good deal of money. I should sell it if I were you. It is not in keeping. Perhaps it seems to you a trifle not worth mentioning, but you remember what Walter Pater says about some trifling and pretty graces being insignia of the nobler world of aspiration and idea."

Miss Markham clasped her hands. "How strange," she said. "I was reading that just as you came in. How strange that you should have known it!"

"My dear lady, you must not imagine that I am a romantic man, for I am not, nor am I a good man. I am not highly connected, and I have not got a better self; the only self I have got is the one before you. But I do claim to be able to appreciate. I have appreciated this evening immensely. Walter Pater is not the last word just now, but I have always appreciated beautiful prose. Far more than beautiful prose I appreciate the pure poetry of your own temperament." He raised his glass. "To your good health, Miss Markham, and good night."

As he neared the door, she called him back. "You have forgotten the pearls," she said.

"No, but I wanted you to remind me."

She unclasped them, and handed them to him. He held them in his hand for a moment. "They are warm," he said, "from your soft, round neck." He raised them to his lips for a moment and then dropped them into a prosaic inside pocket of his coat.

"Yes," he said, "from time immemorial women have been fond of casting their pearls before swine, haven't they? But you have kept the real pearls." He bowed low to her, and in a moment was gone.

In a letter which Miss Markham wrote to Miss Ryles appeared the following passage:

"It was such a pity, dear, that you could not come down to the bungalow the other week-end, it was so quiet and peaceful; incidentally, by mere chance, I met quite the most charming man I have ever seen in my life. No more news, except that I got tired of my old pearl necklace and am getting another.

"Oh, and I was quite forgetting; you said that if ever I wanted to part with my emerald ring, I was to give you the first refusal of it. My dear, you can have it. I have decided that pearls are the only things I can wear."

Naturally Miss Markham had to give notice to the police of the fact that she had lost her pearl necklace.

She had heard something moving in her bedroom, and on entering it a man had jumped out through the window. All she could say for certain was that he was clean-shaven, and had close-cropped black hair.

Printed in Great Britain
by Amazon

37914175R10079